CHRIS MALONE

#ISOLATE

Chris Malone

#isolate

CHRIS MALONE

Content compiled for publication by Richard Mayers of *Burton Mayers Books*.
Cover design by Martiella Design

First published by Burton Mayers Books 2021.
All rights reserved.

A CIP catalogue record for this book is available from the British Library

ISBN: **978-1-8383459-8-3**

Typeset in **Garamond**

www.BurtonMayersBooks.com

DEDICATION

#isolate is dedicated to mavericks and trailblazers.

~ CONTENTS ~

ACKNOWLEDGMENTS

Many thanks to my publisher, Richard Mayers, for his continuing support, to my beta readers Liz van Santen, Pam Jarvis and Vicky Ball, to Heather Malone for her encouragement, and to my husband Ken.

'We have gone so far down the slippery slope of *progress*, that we all now need to call a halt. We are slaves to technology, we are polluting our planet at an alarming rate, and too many of our leaders are concerned with lining their own pockets rather than enabling hardworking citizens to thrive. Even more astounding is the emerging evidence that responsibility for the glitch lay, not with cyber-terrorists, not with the #isolators, but *with our own government*. Friends, there is a way forward ...'

Robin FitzWilliam, summer 2025

PRELUDE

So who did #stoptheglitch? For a short while, my adversary Robin FitzWilliam claimed to have succeeded, but the morning after her return to Caernef camp, Gid, one of her raggle-taggle gang of co-conspirators, shattered the peace. I was informed that Gid ran down to the folly and told *her* that the glitch was back, that their phones had started screaming again.

Since that moment, widespread public anger prompted by the glitch has pushed more and more citizens to turn their backs on the establishment. Alternative communities called earths, are being created by stealth, down muddy paths, taking advantage of relaxed planning restrictions. Attempts at self-sufficiency are gaining ground alongside a counter-culture of urban homeworking. People are sticking two fingers up at the life which let them down, and joining #isolate. Isolate from society. Isolate from the power games which use loaded dice. Isolate with people who they trust. Hide and thrive. Protect and survive.

But I'm not a supporter of the earths, or the runners who connect them.

People call me Miranda. I am the most feared of Robin's close companions. Back in 2022 we fled the glitch together, but subsequently became rivals, and bitter enemies. Working for Reginald De Vere, now I am investigating the possibility that responsibility for the glitch does lie, in fact, as the government claims, with Robin's maverick #isolators. They do, after all, hope to disrupt twenty-first century capitalist society. But their supposed bottom line is

1

integrity, so something doesn't hang together. Reginald has tasked me with finding out whether Robin is as squeaky clean as she presents. Trouble is, I'm handling my own problems just now.

RUNNERS AT DUSK

I have made a huge mistake. Not the sort of mistake which can be marked with red pen and sorted, but a life-changing, potentially devastating and stupid error. I cannot admit to it, or my credibility will fail, but I simply have to tell someone. I need to get it off my chest. All I need is your ears. By telling you, I will settle the oil so that a layer of pure gold forms on the top of the thick murk. Clarity.

Despairing at my momentary lack of judgement, self-loathing fills my cavities. I am usually so intuitively precise. I am careful, while cleverly impulsive. But I will no longer be their first choice when they inevitably discover what I actually did yesterday, before rushing out here and ending up the damp and dirty spy. As I crouch in this godforsaken gulley under shelter of autumn leaves, still clinging on to the accursed twigs I ache with indecision.

Peering through the criss-crossing black lines I can barely discern the parade ground, but I remembered to shove my small digital monocular in my pocket before I fled, slipping noiselessly away from my London persona.

The runners are assembling under the floodlights, buzzing with an electric urgency. Usually masked, here barefaced, they do not often get to actually meet, from what I hear. This appears to be a jubilant clandestine gathering. The place is so remote that they think they are safe, not knowing that I got wind of their activities. I visited this camp a couple of years ago, when the glitch was originally an issue. In fact, we took it over for a couple of days, before Karl was cruelly despatched by a clumsy arm of the security

3

services. Karl understood. He believed in re-setting humanity with an intellectual fervour, which captured my mind at the time. Bastards. I remember telling Robin, on a bizarre steam train excursion, that Karl's gang simply wanted the glitch to wipe capitalism out completely. I told her the far left was hiding in the far right, that politics was messed up, but she didn't listen. What would Karl advise me to do now?

I can smell worms and feel insects scurrying under stones before the darkness of the night finally engulfs us. I cannot hear the sea, although I feel its brooding presence down the hill and over the cliff. Pressing my body into the hollow, sculpted by aeons of wind, rain and creatures, shivers pass down my arms. The flak jacket warms my core, but my legs are numb with damp. Stealthily, I pull my gloves from my jeans' pocket I peer through the lens and zoom on to their makeshift staging, where preparations are still in train. I can discern the lean, fit outlines of the young and fearless, eager to hear from their unlikely middle-aged leader: my erstwhile companion, Robin.

Yes, I am subconsciously postponing coming clean with you, I will speak softly, although the runners are some distance from my hiding place.

I was, as usual, supremely in command, having fulfilled my brief, and more. Pleasing Reginald De Vere, the puppet-master, so that he took me into the back rooms of The Covert Inn. I was drinking Club Soda with lime, keeping my head clear, when Reginald introduced me to an old school-friend, Rupert, who happens to occupy a senior role in the Civil Service. When Reginald made his excuses, seeking an 'early night', surreptitiously sliding my instructions to me as he rose from the table, I instinctively knew what he was asking me to do.

While Rupert conversed with a group behind us, I checked the note, but all that it said was 'HE KNOWS'.

Reginald and I dance effortlessly between the establishment and the worlds of renegades and rebels. Or I should say 'danced'. Well-practised at extracting information, casually, from older suited men who can be flattered into indiscretions, I launched my offensive, shrouding my questions in the banter of flattery, not realising that in Rupert, I might have had met my match. As the night wore on, he began to slip casually audacious questions into the mix, and realising that I would not play ball, he made to leave. Not to be outperformed, I adjusted my approach, razor-sharp. Fuelled by the Club Soda. Rupert's vision, however, was beginning to cloud over. He persisted, calling me, with a genial sneer, 'one of Reginald's cocottes.' Tapping on his phone, he boasted, in his received pronunciation, '*Another* young woman needs me this evening.' I stood my ground, unmoved. Locked in a form of subterfuge and mental combat, we continued. Adrenalin, and a frisson which teetered on the edge of the truth, fired me up. I began to realise that he knew I knew that he *knew*, and that I would stop at nothing to find out. Each time I nettled him, I noted that his fingers returned almost imperceptibly to his trouser pocket.

'Thank you for your company tonight, which has been most … revealing,' he goaded, his hand, again, in the pocket.

'The night is still young,' I remember floundering, seeking an invitation rather than a let-down. Reginald said that Rupert 'knew'. I needed to 'know' too: desperately. To discover the real source of the glitch would not only ensure my career but could be world-changing.

He rose, a touch unsteadily, and I helped him on with his too-tight slim-fit wool overcoat, picking off a silver hair and running my fingers across his shoulders. He reciprocated, taking my arm. So far, so good. We walked through the rear lounge, our legs brushing, continuing the competitive banter. We emerged into the street, bustling with nocturnal revellers, but this is where things began to deteriorate. Someone else was interested in Rupert.

There were only a few seconds between the door of The Covert Inn and Rupert's chauffeured car, which drew up on cue. All I know is that it was a female, dressed like one of Robin's runners, but obviously known by Rupert. She knocked against him, an old trick, and in that split second, I was able to slide my hand into the pocket, discover a small digital device, and secrete it up my sleeve.

I smiled benevolently, thanked him for a pleasant evening, as his attention shifted to the runner, and I disappeared into the night. I had got there before her.

. . . .

The assembled runners are being drawn forwards as a band takes the stage, to open the event. There are several hundred raw and toned would-be heroes. Through the monocular, I focus on the woman preparing to play lead guitar. She tunes up, now in the spotlights, and then she blasts the clifftop air, joined by the rebellious beat of the young en masse.

She's good. Her echoing solo pierces the air, trembling in my ears.

As I was saying, I messed up, for the first time in my career. Maybe the last. I blame the cat. The digital device turned out to be a miniscule flash drive on a keyring. No keys. I was keen to read it, and having hailed a cab, dashed back to my secure and unobtrusive rented room in Golders Green. I unearthed an adaptor which enabled me to open the files on the tiny silver stick. No encryption, and no password. I couldn't believe that I was straight in, but the contents were disappointing. My heightened expectations were dashed, as I viewed the sparse spreadsheet showing a list of dates. They could be birthdays, or something completely irrelevant to my investigations.

I soon realised that they were not birthdays, but a list of twenty-two glitches in the most recent two years, since the major world-wide glitch. Also several dates in the forthcoming months.

You're right though, my catastrophic error was more titillating than stealing someone's flash drive. Determined to make sense of the dates, I decided to head for Reginald, despite the hour. I didn't text him, as he was bound to be asleep at this unearthly time of the night. He knew more about Rupert than I did, and we generally operate far more effectively together than apart. I took the night bus, incognito. The seats smelt of the regulars, littering the aisle with their meagre belongings. By four in the morning, I was standing under a street light in the drizzle, outside Reginald and Cynthia's Hampstead mansion.

I seethe with fury as I remember the moment. An early night: the liar! Reginald is … was … decent. He and I shared everything. It was the only way to keep our heads above the dangerous parapet along which De Vere Stratagems trod. He paid me well: very well, plus provided the Golders Green accommodation, and Summertown, but more important was our equity. He shook my hand in his quaint pseudo-old-fashioned way, and we were in it together.

Usually extremely careful, last night he let himself down, maybe due to passion, or bravado. The curtains of the front lounge were only partially drawn. The lights were low, but sufficient to reveal all to an unexpected onlooker. No doubt Cynthia, the wronged-wife, was asleep upstairs.

I've deposed dictators. I've travelled undercover through enemy territory and rescued rebel leaders. I've solved the insoluble and come out on top *every* time. I have, albeit briefly, even represented constituents in The House. But now you will see that I've blown all this, with one fucking stupid act. The rest of my life, for what it is, will now have to be dedicated to righting the wrong, and I don't know how. Yet.

So many times, I have told trainees never to act in revenge. Lie low. Wait, gain control, plan ahead, and then act in cold blood. Turn any negativity into creative power. Triumph.

It sounds pathetic when I tell you out loud what I did when I saw their two semi-naked bodies through the curtains, his face clearly identifiable, even without his glasses, entangled, upright, with a spotty intern from the Minister's department. Disgusting. I hope the secrets that he squeezed out of her were worth it. Once I had that killer image on my phone, I ... don't even ask ... and then I left as quickly and quietly as I had arrived.

Just before the milkman reached the grand gateposts, a black cat dashed out from the bushes and nearly tripped me, which aggravated my mood. I blame the cat that I'm in this mess. At the bus stop, in a fit of madness, I focused on my phone, my eyes smarting from tiredness. I accessed Reginald's personal account through the back door, posed as him, and posted the image, adding a brief caption, "How to solve the glitch". Then I turned my phone off.

I took another night bus home. It was empty most of the way and I felt exultant, euphorically drunk on my dirty achievement, and tiredness. Running through my mind the way that my action would compromise the smarmy old git, I began to realise that I had always sought to outsmart him. How dare he deceive me, especially when he and I had been so squeaky clean. He sent me off to extract trade secrets from other men's beds readily enough. On reflection, maybe that was why.

I persuaded myself that he had never valued me, that he *used* me as his fit female. I lived the dream as his enigmatic femme fatale. I simply will not be used by him any longer.

The sun was rising over the rooftops when I arrived home, damp and determined. There wasn't time to eat, or to sleep. I switched on the laptop and held my head in disbelief as already, I read, *Account deleted* plus a degree of media noise, naming Reginald. The tabloids were onto it like cadaverous vultures. It was too late to undo my action. And the woman ...

I didn't answer my phone as he tried repeatedly to reach me. I packed up, destroyed most of the evidence of my occupation of the small room, stashing a few key pieces of kit in a box and labelled it 'for collection', dropped the key through the landlady's letterbox and left, my previously buoyant mood totally destroyed as I realised the full import of my stupid, stupid action.

You couldn't do my job if you were sentimental or even too moral. I didn't despair, but I took myself in hand. My reliably tough outer shell holding firm, I knew where to head, out to Caernef Camp. I had discovered earlier in the day, before my ridiculous lapse, that the runners were to assemble for a rare briefing. I hadn't even told Reginald as there was no privacy at The Covert Inn, and he left before I had a chance to report back. Now I know why he left; the Tosser.

Here at Caernef, the beat of drums resonates between the low wooden buildings, hundreds of young faces turn towards the stage. A haunting riff of guitar ties the crowd together and they roar with applause, while I crouch in the damp and slimy ditch. Robin marches out on to the boards and has to calm the riotous ovation. They are using an old PA system, and her strident words travel faintly across to my cold ears:

'Friends, heroes, runners: you are ensuring the future of the planet, and we salute you.'

. . . .

I listen attentively to Robin's impassioned speech, desperate to glean secrets, and to understand more of this weird eco-world of counter-culture. She talks of the vital role played by the runners in connecting diverse communities. She names individuals and they come on to the stage to rapturous applause, receiving trophies, which they hold high, waving triumphantly to the clapping mass. She moves on to extol the virtues of their electric fleet: the hundreds of eco-vehicles donated to their cause by Greenerwheels, a burgeoning multi-national with an eye for opportunity, and key to the success of the runners across the whole of the UK.

Her tone changes, and she shifts to focus on democracy, spouting idealistic platitudes, which they seem to like. When she mentions sabotaging ballot papers, my ears prick up. This is new ground, and is of particular interest to me. 'If we cannot turn the tide through the ballot box, we are compelled to express our disgust with those ruining our society, to demonstrate the strength of feeling of so many citizens. We owe it to our fellow human beings ...' The applause and cheering drown her final words, and the band strikes up while she walks down among the runners, and they touch her clothing as if she is some fucking god-sent saint. I huddle into the tree-roots picking my nails in frustration. I have discovered nothing here so far.

Nathan, Robin's sycophantic university drop-out, obviously selects the runners for their blind loyalty and their fitness levels. He takes to the stage with an act of deference, and organises an activity, like a trainee teacher. They form groups, passing round beer bottles, but their voices are too low so that I cannot catch their words. Time for me to move.

While their attention is focused elsewhere, I slip stiffly out from my hiding place and make my way forwards with stealth to the nearest of the wooden dormitories. In the open, in the half-light, I can see the sea way below. A tiny flashing light is illuminating the water in bursts. I stick to the shadows, and am now within touching distance of the building. I reach the veranda. As I guessed, everyone is over by the stage. The door to the dormitory is ajar. In a split second I am inside, smelling the cedar.

I stand in silence, listening, quickly confirming that the room is empty, and the bunks unoccupied. Running my hands through rucksacks, I find what I seek, runner's garb, more or less in my size. Sleek glittering suit, cloak and hood with face mask. It takes no longer than a few minutes to jettison my damp clothes and to squeeze into the uniform of the runners, to transfer my meagre belongings into my new pockets, and to stuff my discarded clothing into my backpack, folding the flak jacket carefully. But I cannot find one of their adapted phones. Emerging from the dormitory I blend into the adored company of runners.

Joining one of the groups, it takes a while for me to acclimatise. Listening, nodding, grinning when they grin, I discover the beer is non-alcoholic and join in their communal drinking. Passing the bottle round is a flagrant breach of etiquette these days. Their fighting talk and youthful enthusiasm is naively alluring, for its superficiality. They are preparing a nationally-coordinated attack strategy. The group leader is speaking very quickly, asking loads of questions. The runners answer, throwing suggestions into the ring. One types on a laptop and the others sync on their phones. I am trying to link my phone to their system, but failing, so feign participation. I don't learn anything until they start talking about the glitch.

'What's our backup plan if there is another glitch?'

'They are bound to target us if they get wind of ...'

'So you reckon the glitches are targeted then?'

'Course they are.'

'If there is a glitch, we switch to emergency mode. We've done it before.'

'It helps in some ways: means they aren't focused on us.'

'Ha, that'll show them. They try to disrupt us and end up strengthening us!'

Cheers follow. Their sleek bodysuits and soft protective cloaks mean they are indistinguishable from each other in the darkness of the late evening. I am immersed in a brainwashed gang of renegades, all dancing to Robin's tune.

They largely ignore me, and preferring to stay under the radar, I slip off into the shadows, before Nathan arrives to debrief.

I wander quietly through the groups of runners, their bodies sparkling, while my ears strain for clues as to their next steps. A young girl is eagerly collecting the empty beer bottles, dropping them one by one into in wooden crates, darting from group to group. They all know her; runners ruffle her hair and grin as she weaves through their legs. I drain the bottle which was passed to me half-empty, and call her over. She scurries across and throws me an engaging smile. As I hand her my empty, I quiz her, 'Caernef is busy tonight?'

'But by tomorrow lunchtime they will have all gone, and we will get the camp ready for Monday morning.'

'More schools in?'

'Yep. Which group of runners are you in?'

'I'm with them,' I point, satisfying her, adding, 'we're planning for the voting …'

'Yes, it will be good.'

'I can't see it working?'

Her dark eyes twinkle as she tells me how convinced she is that the plot to shame the government will lead to change, her wisdom beyond her years. I tease as much out of her as I can, gently, amiably, and she tells me emphatically, 'It will work. My Mum and Dad will refuse to vote. Lots of other people will join in. They are going to let me stay up late to see all the announcements; there'll be millions of spoiled votes.'

'You'll only see it if there's no glitch.'

'Haha,' she laughs, chanting, 'We are going to stoptheglitch. We are going to stoptheglitch. We are going to stoptheglitch,' And she drifts off into the throbbing darkness to collect more empties.

So, it seems that Robin and her runners are coordinating a massive protest vote in the forthcoming General Election, not to skew the outcome, but to gain publicity for their cause. Not sure how that will stop the glitches.

The band is striking up again, and the runners are gathering below the stage. The floodlights, powered by solar generators, reflect on the iridescent fabric cladding the crowds.

I have nearly forgotten Reginald, my old boss, and my stupid indiscretion amid the hubbub of the clifftop. I have moved on. Reginald is dead to me: I work for myself now. Being a free agent suits me better.

With everyone focused on the event, I decide to pay a visit to the folly out on the clifftop; Robin's famous home, which was intended as a retreat from society, but has been transformed into an internationally recognised symbol of rebellion. I haven't actually been right down there in person before, but have studied the maps, and seen the photographs all over the news and social media. Ironic that a place intended as an escape from society has ended up splashed across the tabloids.

Now dressed as a runner, I start to understand how they feel, sleek and cleverly camouflaged, whether in cities or out in the open. The very tightness and lightness of the fabric empowers the wearer, the hood is designed to protect and to anonymise, with a comfortable mask which can be raised over the face when needed. And the cloak adds warmth as well as covering your contours: genius. Sleek genderless fashion. If I was ten years younger, I might be tempted to join the runners, undercover of course. Last year Reginald planted one, Hayden, but he went native, drawn in by the persuasive power of Robin and her gang. A lost asset.

I skirt a small wood, which provides shelter, autumn leaves rustling in the breeze, and I head down across some rough grassland, past the cottage, which I remember. I reach a clifftop path, checking behind, ears and eyes alert.

The folly looms on the horizon, chunky yet elegant, now a symbol for disrupters. But for me, Caernef is a memory of times gone and people lost. This lookout surveys the national political landscape as much as the calming estuary.

It takes longer than I imagine to prize open the small window at the back. I slide inside, clambering down into a tiny kitchen and losing no time. Replacing my winter gloves with disposables, and using my headtorch, I search systematically, moving through the tiny rooms, looking for papers, equipment, clues or incriminations. I have searched so many dark offices through the last decade, but tonight I only find squirrelled seeds, nuts, and poems written in long-hand on scraps of paper.

There is nothing of interest. The romance of this pokey place doesn't work for me other than giving me an intimate insight into the very ordinary woman who lives here, uses toothpaste, drapes clothes over the back of a chair, and spills coffee going up the steep stairs. About to leave with my tail between my legs, my phone vibrates, detecting subversive digital signals. Odd?

Returning to the place where it triggered, upstairs by the window seat, I stare into the blackness which must transform into a serene vista by day. My phone triggers again. I look at the screen and it confirms that I am very near to something which causes a digitally disruptive signal. A glitch? The source of a glitch?

Pausing with bated breath I hear noises outside. Damn! Two figures are standing out on the clifftop, talking, turning towards the only door into the folly. Hastily descending the stairs, I reach the kitchen window as they turn the key, slither through and close it, silently. Unable to latch it, I dive into the undergrowth and pause, my heart reverberating in my ribcage. I decide I need to get back to my car and put some distance between me and this weird place.

My identity largely concealed by the excellent runner's clothing, I squirm out of the cover of the bushes, and walk boldly back up the field. The echo of guitar wafts across the greasy tussocks, along with the excited burble of young voices. It is too late to take cover by the time I see a figure approaching me through the blackness, and so I brazen it out, striding with confidence.

But it is Robin.

'Evening,' I volunteer.

She stares into my eyes, double-takes, and whispers, with incredulity 'Miranda?'

OAK APPLES

I run, instinctively, uphill through the darkness, across the parade ground and out to the road, where the tarmac is a relief underfoot. I should have stayed and questioned her, and chide myself at missing such an opportunity.

I reach my car which skulks in a layby near the train station. The comfort of an illuminated dashboard spurs me on, as my key is recognised, the engine purrs, and I travel far too fast along the narrow lanes until I am well-clear of any chance pursuers.

Got to get away from this godforsaken place on to decent roads. I know that it will be a couple of hours before I hit the motorway. As tens of miles are eaten up by the empty tarmac, I drift. Opening the window for a blast of air to keep me awake, I play back my experience at the camp. The occasional headlights of midnight vehicles blast my eyeballs.

Okay, I've walked out of the best-paid job I've ever had, and compromised my contacts, but the burden of guilt is becoming lighter by the mile. Finally free of constraints, I realise that I can go where I choose. I could go home. Perhaps I should jack it all in and get a proper day job, preserve my health and meet a stable partner, rather than hurtle from here to there. That's if they don't charge me for my arrant stupidity.

The sleek runners-clothing feels empowering, and I hit ninety on the straight stretches, returning to the idea of turning double-agent in Robin's troops. I can match their pace. But I realise that Robin knows me too well. She knows my eyes, the scars on my wrists, the beginnings of wrinkles on my forehead. Vulnerability. *Steer clear of runners Miranda, be yourself, stay clean and solve the mystery of the glitch single-handed. You will ensure a comfortable retirement before you hit forty.*

The next thing I know is the massive overhead signs on the M5 telling me to slide off to the left towards London. God, I have reached the M42 on automatic pilot. Can't even remember Birmingham. I grit my teeth for a few more miles, and swerve into the services, where I cut the engine and sit for a moment in the silence. The half-empty car park, the glare of lights, drive thru and the Tesla supercharger open at all hours. Just as I free myself from my seatbelt, my phone goes off.

It is Reginald. Again.

Totally absorbed in the journey, and fighting exhaustion, I had forgotten about him. Loads of missed calls, and a message. I stick it on speaker, and hear his now pathetic tones, 'Meredith, I need you to check in. There have been some … complications this end … but all is now under control. Anyway, make sure to pick up some coffee on your way in. Thanks. Bye for now.'

'Pick up some coffee' is our emergency code. It means get back to base at all costs.

Reginald sounds calm, certainly not accusing me of *the* misdemeanour. Perhaps I've got away with it this time. I'm pretty sure no one saw me. Maybe I should go back to base after all. Slamming the car door, it locks behind me, and I head for the washroom in the services, my rucksack on my back. Not one of the bleary-eyed travellers flinches, as a runner dives into the cubicle, transforming into an ordinary late-thirties woman, in jeans and jumper.

Cold water on my face, my fingers raking through my hair, I brush my teeth, vigorously. The ritual of the minty scrub. Cleaning my thoughts, trying to erase the memories of Reginald, semi-naked through the curtains, without his glasses.

The runners are bribed with just-legal drugs to stay

awake. They take all sorts, which Robin's collaborators obtain in bulk from China. Fuck their squeaky-clean eco-image. I looked into that last year for Reginald. I am sorely tempted, but learnt at an early age that you are better off relying on your own resources than any of the alluring stimulants lurking in the black market. I could get them if I wanted, but pride myself in my principles. Ha! Principles.

Overnighters like me in the café, grabbing coffee. I use Reginald's card, decaf tea and an almond croissant. He will be able to track my location, if he is mindful to find me, but who cares. I have no cash on me, and my own cards are back home.

I perch on a stool at the coffee bar. After a night out on the cliffs, poking in other people's sordid lives, I need blood sugar. I also need sleep, and decide to head for Oxford. Haven't been home for weeks, and simply want to be able to shut a door and be inside somewhere normal.

On to the M40, and still no dawn. Holding my eyelids open with sheer willpower and wondering whether to cut and run, or to return to Reginald, I put my foot down. Hurtling past Banbury on to the A34, past the slumbering Park & Ride, and into Summertown. That unmistakable ecstasy of coming home, parking up on the drive. The key in the door, the smell of stuffy rooms, mail on the doormat. Heading for bed, passing a small brown packet in the pile of post, I hover, and my phone starts going nineteen to the dozen. It is detecting subversive signals, just like in the folly.

It will have to wait until daylight, when I can wear gloves and do it properly. Novichok stories tell me it's not worth the risk now, especially when I am dog tired.

The sheets are stale, and the bedroom air fetid, but I'm too shattered to care, and I sleep.

....

"Mars" booms out of my phone, from "The Planets" ringtone cycle, and I jolt myself awake, relieved to be in my own bed after months of snatched nights kipping down in Reginald's rented Golders Green hideaway.

But as I fumble for my phone, the leaden weight of guilt returns. They might discover today that I am the person to drag into the cells. Pushing these thoughts well clear of my waking mind, I glean some pleasure from re-establishing myself in the comfortable detached house which I call home. In reality, the house is a grace-and-favour allowance from a grateful former client who is dodging tax and needs a long-term investment. There is no contract. Each time I return, I half-expect to see tenants, squatters, or boards over the windows while assets are being seized, but my affluent refuge has remained unnoticed for several years, so I trust in its security as much as I trust in anything.

My phone alarm is in overdrive as I pass the pile of mail on the sideboard. Collecting gloves from the kitchen, I gingerly place the small packet on a chopping board. Tempted to rip it open, I stop myself. Instead, I postpone the moment, shower, slide into a clean set of clothes, and organise a makeshift breakfast of sardines, stale biscuits and green tea. I sip while studying the padded bag.

It is addressed to me, which is unusual, as I keep this address private. The off-duty me resides here. It is not Reginald's handwriting, or that of his demure secretary. The printing is in capitals, attempting to conceal the identity of the person who, I assume, packed this little communication.

Unable to put the moment off any longer, I don my protective glasses, and cradle the packet in my gloved hands, feeling for clues, before slitting the top in one deft stroke. Nothing happens, but my phone continues to detect the disruptive signal, stronger now. I open the top of the envelope, which grins at me, but see no letter, no gifted digital drive, no high-tech offering. Instead, a small spherical object, like a Malteser, rolls out, and on to the floor.

Instinctively, I scoop it up, along with fluff and crumbs, and place it on a saucer, where I examine it. Heavy, and the size of a small hazel nut, it is made out of dark wood. It seems oddly familiar. Despite the angry bleeping, I hold my phone magnifier over it and examine the smooth surface.

All that interests me is a minute dot of filler. Something has been embedded in this wooden marble. Unable to discover more, I protect it with the padded bag and zip it securely in the pocket of my rucksack.

Puzzled, I sit in silence, recalling recent events, my energy focused on whether to respond to Reginald's plea to return to base. While I watch the cat from next door stalking a robin, under the laurel bushes, I think again of the script on the package. The robin flies off, and the cat cleans its whiskers. I retrieve the printed handwriting sample and stare at it.

It is addressed to Meredith Brenton, my real name, not Miranda, which is the pseudonym I use when working for Reginald. Odd. The sender obviously wants to detach me from the old fox. I run through my routine of mental exercises, relax muscles, close eyes.

Clock ticking the time away, cat and bird in garden. Minutes pass.

I emerge from my trance, take a jar from the spice rack, tip the contents down the sink and sluice them away with a gush. A strong aroma of cinnamon makes me sneeze as I remove the small wooden sphere from the packet and place it safely in the jar, clicking the lid shut and stashing it in my rucksack.

Turning to the packet, I check that the removal of the ball has eliminated any signal, and then dismantle the padded layers. About to give up on this vain search for a message from the sender, I finally spy a scrap of paper secreted in the wadding. On one side, printed in miniscule letters, I read 'HE KNOWS,' and on the other side 'AK'.

I realise instantly that this must be a message from the undercover runner, who Reginald told me had gone native, and it is clearly intended for me. 'AK,' stands for *Anna Karenina,* and is a signal that the sender of the message is, or was, in Reginald's trusted inner circle. The old copy of the novel still sits on Reginald's bookshelf, and serves as a receptacle for communications from those of us who come and go at De Vere Stratagems. And HE is, of course, not simply 'he', not Reginald, or Rupert, but Hayden Eckley, the undercover runner.

Shit! I may have been so close to him last night at Caernef. Another missed opportunity. I pick the wadding apart, but in vain, as nothing else is concealed there. Ever careful, I burn the remains of the package in the grate, and grab a bite to eat before I leave.

I ignore yet another message from Reginald, who is, I expect, becoming frustrated; a curt text this time, "Remember coffee."

. . . .

Locating Hayden has taken days. Deliberately avoiding Reginald, I worked it out alone, and have secured a meeting, which Hayden assures me is in a safe location, at a remote runner's bothy. Having driven for a couple of hours, I am parking in a tourist spot, and am about to travel the final half-mile on foot. As with many of their meeting places, the sat nav doesn't take you there. I don't know how they operate with no signal at all, despite civilisation being just over the hill.

Locking my hopefully unobtrusive silver Nissan in a car park used by ramblers and dog-walkers, I set off along one of the routes clearly worn by runners, and marked with their characteristic ®, branded on the gatepost. These networks of footpaths and bridleways are now used more than ever before, as Robin's subterranean army marches across the countryside, delivering, planning and plotting. They say it's above board. The exponential growth of her followers is astounding. No doubt it will be studied by sociologists as the phenomenon of the mid-2020s. A kick-back protest movement. A rallying post-pandemic cry against insensitive government and prolonged austerity. Ironically, I am comfortable with her ideals, but would never admit it out loud.

Breaking into a jog, I feel like a runner. Route imprinted on my memory, checking behind, scanning ahead. Well-trodden greensand underfoot, heather bushes and sporadic foliage overhead. The smells of forest after rain do nothing for me; I'm no tree-hugger like them.

After ten minutes at pace, I clamber over a stile and into an overgrown field, see a low stone building on the rise, and head for it, even more vigilant. This could easily be a trap; a set-up by Robin to get her own back after I appeared at Caernef. Or Hayden might be seeking the glory of having enticed me. I check, but there is no phone signal, even for my multi-ranger. Vulnerability. Silence. I pause in the shade of the wall, rough stones and crumbling mortar, checking the Smith and Wesson hidden under my jacket. No mistakes this time. Patience. I'm early.

The runners came from nothing. Suddenly they were in the news, you saw them on the streets, on foot and in their trendy eco-vehicles. They profess to be an above-board legal movement, but I know better. She attracts all sorts as runners; mostly young and unemployed, students earning on the side, protestors, eco-warriors, people ranging from disaffected has-been socialists to libertarians, to conspiracy theorists, appalled by the impact of an increasingly intolerant and dictatorial government. Reminds me of the reasons behind my brief stretch in Westminster, before I met Reginald. The runners are paid a basic wage and receive incentives depending on what they deliver. Hayden described these enticements to us before he 'went native': food, accommodation, supplies from sponsors like fair trade coffee and ethical beer, the best boots money can buy, and of course, the bodysuits, sports underwear, hoods and masks, made from secret eco-weave. Then there are the gigs and the meetings. All designed to attract the idealistic young in a post-pandemic world.

It is possible that Reginald misinterpreted Hayden's stance. Not sure what to think of the guy … yet.

I check my surroundings, sinking as far into the shadows as I can, listening.

Of course, even more interesting are the communities

that they serve, the off-grid #isolate back-to-nature brigade, and the home-workers determined to circumvent the giants of capitalism, despite the challenges of ongoing localised glitches.

The secret behind these persistent temporary glitches, involving the failure of digital services, sometimes power as well, is unknown, at least publicly. The unanswered question on the lips of the person in the street is who, or what, is responsible? The Government wants us to believe it is #isolate.

The runners are the go-betweens, hallowed and lauded connectors. They started off conveying eco-produce between areas, both small-scale domestic and from agribusiness. This expanded to general bartering, swaps, books, anything which can be carried. No wonder eBay and Amazon filed lawsuits, as Robin's networking has already massively reduced their market share. Suddenly Britain was re-establishing itself at the top of the international pecking order for ingenuity and innovation. A counter-culture to be proud of. Unprecedented empowerment. And completely down to Robin, masterminding it all out on the clifftop at Caernef. Bizarre.

I hear the distant soft pad of running feet, but detect more than one person approaching. Immediately on the offensive, I slide round the corner from where I can view the approach to the bothy. Hayden crests the rise, drawing to a halt, followed by a companion, a woman, I think, who stays at a distance. That wasn't in our agreement. I have come alone and he has compromised my trust before we have even begun.

He stands immobile, as they are trained to do, listening. A man with long hair escaping from his eco-suit, his bushy beard giving him a Viking look. He is followed by a typical female runner, hair short, androgynous, compact. I don't know how he detects my presence as I am still as stone, but he walks confidently round to me, his hand outstretched, beaming.

'Meredith … Miranda. It is great to see you again.'

'You said alone.'

'Oh, yes, this is Jade, my shadow. She goes everywhere with me at the moment, not perhaps the toilet, or the shower, but everywhere else.'

'The bed?'

'Haha, no, but not far off!'

I whisper, 'Hayden, prove to me you are still on-side. Reginald said …'

'Come into the bothy,' he gestures towards the stone building. The woman moves closer and smiles at me.

'I'd prefer to stay out here.'

He detects my irritation, and responds petulantly, hissing under his breath, 'I sent you an oke didn't I?'

'What the fuck is an oke? Some wooden Malteser for kids to play with. Doesn't tell me anything.'

'Miranda! Do you know what they *are*? Worth their weight in gold,' he whispers.

He looks up, then disappears into the trees, while she shrugs her shoulders, and I suddenly remember where I have seen the odd little wooden balls before, in the desk drawer in Robin's folly. I thought they were nuts. I'm missing things.

After a few minutes of Jade and I standing in awkward silence, Hayden stumbles exultantly out of the woodland, and thrusts another small wooden ball into my hand.

'Now this *is* an oak apple!'

It is still attached to the twig, and as I turn it over on my palm, I see a tiny round hole.

'It's a gall, created by the gall wasp,' he explains, adding, 'the hole is where the baby wasp has escaped. The runners use their own fabricated oke apples. Clever isn't it! Instead of the gall wasp larva, there is a micro-computer inside.'

'What the blazes do they do?'

'Hand me your phone …'

'Why?'

'Believe me, you'll see the magic.'

23

I decide I have nothing to lose as there is no signal out here anyway, and pass him the phone.

'You have brought the oke with you?'

Warily, I pull the spice jar out from my rucksack and tip the tiny ball into his cupped hand. He moves close to me, showing me *the magic*. Balancing the wooden sphere in the palm of my hand, he places my phone on my fingers. He doesn't need the password, or to access the encryption. He just enters the back-end with a single swipe. The phone buzzes. He counts briskly to ten, and then shows me the screen. 'Okay, you're connected now. You should receive all runners' messages. There will be signal everywhere. I mean everywhere; underground, abroad, in space maybe, as long as you have this specific oke, your hand, and your phone. Lose one of them, and you're stumped.

'Bloody hell. It's so simple.'

'Yes: that's the joy of it. It is also meant to ride out any glitches, but they haven't perfected that yet. And it's digestible if you want to know. Last week a kid ate one. Turned up in A&E. There was a lot of explaining to do when it was discovered, but it was designed to be safely swallowed by runners if necessary.'

'Good God! Why would anyone want to swallow one?'

'So they could be rescued if captured. We can track the locations of all our runners now.'

Noting Hayden's blatant identification with Robin's side, it dawns on me that they have now hooked my phone into their geo-system. I am trackable, unwillingly transparent and more gullible than I imagined. Once alone, I'll have to jettison the device and sacrifice the intelligence.

Determined to gain something from this rendezvous, I turn to Jade, 'So, how do you find being a runner?'

Blinking shyly at me, her voice is soft, and her look beguilingly trusting. 'It's a great honour, and Hayden is training me well. I'm looking forward to getting out on my own.'

'How were you recruited? It's not a role for every one?'

'Completely by accident. I'm on a gap year and need the money. Some mates were going to a gig and I tagged along. Robin spoke, and it just made so much sense. I want to give back to my country, to make a difference.' She smiles, innocently, and I suppress my frustration at her naivety. I'm not here to lecture.

I refuse to become trapped in the bothy, and we hold a stilted conversation in front of Jade, neither Hayden nor I willing to divulge anything useful. I think he has been sent to tie me into their conspiracy, nothing more. He certainly has no time for Reginald.

'So, Hayden, or should I say HE, what do you "know" then?'

'It's the message everyone is sharing, "HE KNOWS" but no one knows who *he* is!'

Is Hayden bluffing or is he really simply ignorant? Pretending to be grateful for the gift of an oke, I talk about irrelevancies, relieved when he tells Jade they must be moving on. As he makes to run off, he calls to me over his shoulder, 'What about Reginald being caught with his trousers down. Didn't think he could bury that news so easily, but they're all the same. If they know the right people … pity for his *girlfriend* though. She paid the price.'

I can feel the colour drain from my cheeks. Momentarily, my legs tremble, but I resolutely ignore his parting shot, let them go, and warily inspect the inside of the bothy. There is a camera, which I can avoid by sidling round the walls, but as I find nothing, I leave too, the oke rattling in the jar as I run.

. . . .

Judge me if you must, but I returned to the Golders Green flat, unpacked the box abandoned in haste, and took coffee to De Vere Stratagems. I kept my counsel, despite handing Reginald the data stick, which I had slipped from Rupert's pocket, as well as the oke and my phone, which he has replaced. He was thrilled with the oke. For some reason he is fond of Robin. They go back years. He caressed it, marvelling at her ingenuity, and smiling at me, 'Oh Miranda, you never disappoint.' He clearly has no idea.

Now I am dressed in a formal suit, with subtly low-cut blouse, and heels, sitting at the back of a small committee room in Westminster, tagging politely along with a senior civil servant called Algernon, as pretentious as his name. Reginald has presented me to Algernon as a representative from a highly respected digital surveillance company in the pay of the Government. Fortunately, I am not required to speak. Their security is loose, and their trust misplaced. The first hour is spent discussing the national response to the random glitches during the summer. Then, all non-governmental attendees, a dozen of us, are required to leave.

Every time I return to the hallowed corridors, my own Westminster days haunt me. I was heavily into the far left in my late twenties, and was gullible enough to be recruited to stand for Parliament in 2015. Didn't think there was a chance in hell of being elected, which is why I stood, but was elected. Spent a couple of years in the job, and became too tangled in an opposition cybersecurity motion, so resigned immediately prior to the rushed general election. Briefly in the press but off the hook. Made many contacts, and was recruited by Reginald. I learnt loads from the experience, mainly about the hypocrisy.

Algernon nods at me across the room, as a signal for me to leave. Shit. The strap of my bag is caught in the leg of my chair. I yank at the thin, impractical strap, which eventually pings free, but before I exit, I hear him say clearly, 'Well that will keep them quiet. They think we are a load of slipshod old fools. Now on to the real business. We will relocate to my office.'

Interested in the subject matter of this "real business", I hover in the grand doorway long enough to hear the chair of the meeting, a brusque MP in pearls, say to the six remaining attendees, 'Friends, the next part of the meeting will be totally off the record. No phones, no minutes. Algernon will report on the extent to which the glitches are effectively subduing not only the rebels but also the isolators …'

Unable to remain in the room any longer without drawing attention to myself, I slip out and stand, alone, facing the closed door, smiling, as I realise that the speech-to-text function is still playing in the empty corridor.

Aghast, I watch as the words flash up on the screen: "Have you got the figures for us? I want to see fewer runners. I am looking for a reduction in #isolate. These glitches have got to start having impact." Then something about an informal international liaison committee, and a meeting in China of all places.

I see no more, as they decamp.

ZILLAH THE SECOND

As I head for the barriers, at the exit to the street, blithely waving the pass obtained for me by Reginald, I suddenly clock increased security. The pass does retract the barrier, which beeps merrily, but uniformed guards, accompanied by police officers, suddenly encircle me. It is a woman who attempts to arrest me, reciting the spiel for any one rushing through the ticket hall to hear, 'We are arresting you for the murder of Jennifer Hayward ...' Didn't know the name of Reginald's whore: should have told you more about this earlier.

Relying on my split-second reactions, learned as a child in a household of drunks and criminals, I turn. Focused on the small window of escape back through the barrier and out through the alternative exit, I ditch the useless bag and heels, vault, stretch, run. Sending the unsuspecting security guard flying with my fist, I force my way over the barrier, smelling freedom. Outdoor air hits my face as I deftly lose myself in the stream of tourists ambling along the pavement.

Shrill alarms, flashing lights behind me. Shouting. Feet smart as they grate on the rough pavement. I've had to literally run for my life before, and I switch into maximum self-protection mode. I accelerate along the Embankment, causing ripples in the groups of nosey pedestrians. I don't tire. Light breaths, fast legs. Dodging, thinking.

That fucking Reginald set this up. He suggested heels and stiff formal clothing. Oh for a runners' suit right now. Dropping over the wall, I close my eyes momentarily and enter the water. Realising I have nothing on me. No phone, no keys, as instructed. All left with Reginald. Shit.

Distant sirens split the air, wheels on tarmac above, urgent shouting. The water slops, a greyish brown against the rusted iron of a disused barge. Must get to the blind side before they see me. Swim through the thick water. Cold. Duck under the ironwork and reach my goal, spying through riveted girders of old crane to see a swarm of police officers march along the concrete of the jetty, arms waving.

Undetected, soaked and freezing, I quickly explore the barge, discovering a discarded boiler suit, reeking of oil, which I put on, holding my breath to avoid retching from the stink. Grab an iron bar; some sort of handle, and take it with me into the bowels of the boat, where oily water is ankle deep. The rusting floor is already so wet that I don't need to cover my tracks. I locate the furthest point in the cavernous hull, threading my way over and under rusted struts. As the noise of the engine of a motor launch reverberates, I position myself high, obscured. I hang delicately, supporting myself with my arms, my still-bare feet waving desperately seeking a foothold, which I secure, just as torches flash round the interior of the old barge.

'No. No one could have got this far, least of all a woman.'

'Nothing here.'

Aware my bare foot might become visible in the torchlight; I slip it off the girder and clench every muscle in my body.

They linger. I cling on for dear life. Torchlight splashes across the debris, catching the pools of water, reflecting off the oil.

Sound of boots retreating. Reassuring putter of motor launch. Silence. Beautiful and blessed silence. Arm muscles pulling like strings about to snap.

But I am not alone.

I hear someone scrambling up the side of the barge, the shuffle of feet, and a cough. 'I saw you even if they didn't.' The firm voice of a confident younger man. 'It's okay, I won't turn you in.'

He jumps down into the cavern of twisted iron. A runner. Soaking wet. They get everywhere. I focus on the top of his head, knowing I am unable to hang on much longer.

'I followed you from Westminster. Might be able to help.'

I hang, stock still, holding my breath, counting slowly to override the impulse to drop.

'You can trust me.'

Trust. My mantra; trust no one. Don't even trust myself some days. Like that fateful night outside Reginald's window.

'Well I will just sit here until you come out.'

Why is he doing this? Nothing in it for him. Arm muscles at breaking point. Determined not to give in.

'I could at least fetch you some footwear.'

Shoes are tempting. I so need shoes. Forced to move one of my feet on to a more stable support, he hears the soft rasp of skin on rust, and looks up, but cannot see me in the gloom. That is until he holds his phone high, the blue light dancing off the mess of girders above his head.

With dignity, I hang from my fingertips, and land deftly beside him, black oil squeezing between my toes. 'Hi.'

....

We face each other through the dim and stinking air. Drips and rust.

'I'm Caractacus.'

'And I'm Boudica.'

'Don't believe you.'

'I don't believe you either.'

'Your call, but I am Caractacus. Here, see my phone.' He thrusts a state-of-the-art device into my hand. An image shows the standard runner ID "Caractacus Barnes". I could easily beat him in a fight, but need shoes.

'It's a ridiculous name.'

Thanks! Tell my parents that.' Realising he is no older

than twenty, I smile.

'I saw you rapidly disappearing down the Embankment, no shoes. "That woman will make a good runner" I said to myself, so I followed. Who are you?'

'I'm an undercover agent in a spot of bother. I know Robin personally. Can you find me trainers or boots, size five, and clothes? These overalls stink.'

'Tell you what, seeing as you know Robin – The Robin?'

'Yes.'

'Seeing as you know Robin, I'll leave you with my phone so you know I'll come back. It will take me an hour or so to get home. I can bring stuff in the morning.'

'Tonight.'

'Sorry, can't.'

'Before it gets light?' I plead, trying not to sound as desperate as I feel.

'When's that?'

'7.30. Can you get here about 6am?'

'It's rather early for me. I'll be here by seven.' Looks like I have no choice. He hands me a half-empty flask of water and a soggy KitKat.

'That's all I have on me. Go nowhere. If they come for you, drop my phone overboard and leave a signal. KitKat wrapper on deck or something.'

'Okay. Thanks.' This stripling is telling me how to take care of myself. It is ridiculous, but touching. His naivety tells me more about Robin's runners: inexperienced, idealistic and far too trusting. He leaves, and I hear a neat splash as he drops into the river.

....

I've spent long dark nights in many strange places over the last few years, but nothing like this. The iron creaks, and the water slaps the sides of the barge, so that I am constantly on guard. There is a background reek of oil and muddy slop, and a damp cold is pervading the cluttered hold.

I recall the night I spent with Robin, Nathan, Gid and Eva, locked in a freezing stone chapel. Their ridiculous ideas. They could have been trapped for days had I not picked the lock. That was after the worst glitch. No phones. No power. For days.

Caractacus' phone has a full charge so I can use it as a light, in fact, I'm trying to get in through the rudimentary encryptions. I'm considering phoning a friend, but most of my current contacts are connected with Reginald, and I decide the safest option is to sit it out until morning. If luck is on my side, Caractacus will be true to his word and will return alone at dawn.

I was young and idealistic like him once, but reality kicked in when I had to fend for myself without the protection of an extended family of bizarrely loyal drunks and criminals. Sofa surfing at eighteen, in a strange town, leaving several hated schools behind me, I soon realised that to make something of my life I would need to play catch-up.

In those early days of adulthood, I worked long shifts in bars, and studied at night, through the Open University. Minimal sleep, I was maniacally focused on pulling myself back up to where I should have started. It took more than six years to qualify with a first in a combination of politics and forensic psychology. Doors suddenly opened, which is how I ended up unexpectedly elected to Parliament. Didn't spend long treading those hypocritical out-of-touch corridors as I got tangled up in a cyber scandal. Wasn't a good time. After that, Reginald recruited me, and I became Miranda.

Wash from unseen night-boats slaps against the rusting sides of the barge, troubling my mind. Stock still, listening. But the creaking and grinding of twisted metal simply provides a soporific nocturne, lulling me into semi-consciousness. If I could be more comfortable, I would sleep. Using the phone's light to guide me, I return cautiously to the small wheelhouse on deck, from where I grabbed the stinking boiler suit, and collect some sacking. Alarmed by the demand of busy nocturnal lights on the

Embankment, and not wishing to attract any attention, I return to the bowels of the corroded boat. I tread over dark pools of sticky oil, until I find a dry platform where I curl up hopefully, covering myself with the sacking for warmth, and closing my eyes.

I am unable to sleep, the face of the police officer on repeat, 'We are arresting you for the murder of Jennifer Hayward ...' I never told you that I fired. But it was genuinely intended as a warning shot. Trained in firearms by an ex-SAS renegade, I am always accurate, but it seems I may have been too accurate for my own good this time. Odd. Life-changing. Why am I making mistakes?

Blighted by my past. Bad luck following me around like a bad smell. Was I doomed to criminality right from my first gasping breath, forced into independence before I had learnt how to fend for myself? As a young child, always hungry, and as a teenager, with an in-bred skill to melt into the background. Fuck. I'm better than this. Look at what I have achieved, and look at what I can still achieve. Infatuated with stopping the glitch, with uncovering the real cause. I am so close.

As the midnight hour rolls into one, two and three in the morning, my limbs stiffen, and my brain goes into overdrive. Reginald obviously sent me to the security committee as a method to trap me. That is clear now, but what I overheard was both significant and alarming. The meeting was a front for journalists. It is the *real* meeting afterwards which interests me. A select group of senior parliamentarians are using the glitch to subdue opposition. It is no rebel cyber-terrorist threat. Now I am convinced that the glitch is emanating from the heart of government, because they are using it to force #isolators back into the real world. They want consumers, economically active citizens, not drop-outs, runners and isolators. This is all about money, the state, and the future of society. It is actually about subtle repression; I'm convinced.

The beating of rain on metal above my head is now

overlaying the night-time noises of this creaking hulk. Something soothing in the constant play of the cascading water on the drum of the deck is sending me to sleep. I do not fight it.

'Hey, wakey-wakey Miranda, or should I say Meredith Brenton. Cripes, you look rough. Here!' Caractacus, full of the joys of the morning, somehow knowing all my names, thrusting breakfast up into my hand, a bread roll in a soggy paper bag. Still warm.

'Thank God you're back. That was a long night, but I managed some sleep.'

Is he alone?

'Had to hold it above my head so it didn't get wet. No one saw me, I'm sure, but we can't stay here long. There are eyes out for you everywhere. Saw pictures of you on the BBC.'

'Shit. That's all I need. Are you alone?'

'Course I am.' His young, keen face bobs in the half-light below my small platform. 'You didn't do it did you? Shoot her dead I mean?'

'I fired a single warning shot.' Need to keep to one story: a true story. He raises his eyebrows, and I realise that his hands are empty. All that he has brought for me is a soggy bread roll. Uncomfortable, placing myself in the hands of a kid, I devour the roll and jump on to the pock-marked floor, the rucks of the old boiler suit hanging pathetically off my contours. I hand him his phone, 'Thanks.'

'Now, Miranda my friend, the tide is up. We must swim back across to the bank, unseen, before first light. Strip off that thing. You can't possibly swim in it. There's clothes and kit waiting in an eco-car, with my supervisor, Matt Wolff. This morning we will be whisking you well-clear of London. Come on!'

He watches with curiosity as I peel the boiler suit off, my frozen bare feet stepping daintily on to the oily swill, the smart business suit provided by Reginald hangs in pathetic tatters, rivulets of grey running between my breasts.

Smothering a shiver, I swallow my pride and thank him: 'Caractacus, you're a life-saver.'

Dawn is threatening the horizon. He slips into the water first, then swims with athletic poise, barely discernible, except for his phone. This, he holds above the water line, swimming with his strong legs, his body staying just below the surface. Again, I have no choice but to follow. Deep breath and plunge. Perilously cold, but tranquil water. A strong swimmer, and without the impediment of a phone, I catch and overtake him, hauling myself on to the Embankment with barely a splash. Distant Westminster Pier is bereft of tourists at this unearthly hour, but will have security all over it. We are further up-river, and I see an eco-vehicle hovering. We run, and dive into the car.

....

'Hi Matt,' I say with a false confidence.

'Hi.' As soon as we are in, he puts his foot down. I've never been in one of these things before. Designed for a maximum of two people, Caractacus has taken the passenger seat and I am bundled up in the back, surrounded by packets, where I have to curl my wet arms round my knees to fit. Dripping on their cargo. Why are they doing this? The streets are far from empty even at this hour, and I am conspicuous, but soon realise that the runners are generally revered on the roads. Joggers wave, motorists give them room. Unprecedented.

While Matt and Caractacus talk about the day ahead: their normal delivery routine, I find a large towel in the duffel bag they handed me, and somehow manage to lose the stupid business suit, rubbing myself dry all over, subduing the involuntary bursts of trembling which have been overwhelming me since last night. And there, folded neatly in the bag, is the shimmering suit for a runner. I slip awkwardly and un-modestly into it, aware that the two young guys are watching me in the mirror. Unable to stretch, it's like making a bed in a confined space. There are also shoes. Not what I would buy, but beggars can't be choosers.

Young people's lace-up baseball sneakers. They fit.

Already well out of the centre of the city, warming up, I watch early commuters through the window, and recall my actions on that fated night. I shot to warn. I did not shoot to kill. I'm convinced.

'Okay Miranda, you are a runner now,' Caractacus instructs, 'Matt will be your mentor, just like he mentored me. You will shadow him on the job. I'm off.' The car pulls silently into a bus stop, where Caractacus gets out, waves cheerily and sprints into the distance. My saviour. I'm sad to see him go, but adopt a cold-hearted focus on my next steps.

I quickly hop out of the rear to take the passenger seat. In this split second, dressed as a runner, I could disappear round the corner of the block, but momentarily weighing up options, favour Matt, and fasten the passenger seatbelt.

'I'll be a good pupil. I'm special-forces trained and pretty experienced,' I boast.

Before he slams his foot down again, he turns to me with a steely look. At least ten years older than Caractacus, an unremitting gaze of shrewd eyes. Soft white flecks in his hair, a quizzical curl to his lip.

'Don't know who you have been. I know what they think you've done. Right now, I don't trust your judgement, but I'm gunning for you. I want you to prove your worth. Caractacus is a kind-hearted lad. He's made a strong case for you, but there's much to learn. You can't assume you know it all already. Runners are something different.'

'Why bother to take a chance on me then?'

'To be honest, we're short-staffed at this time in the calendar. Last year's gap students have finished, and with the winter ahead, we need tough recruits. We'll see to the paperwork tonight. Right now, you're in at the deep end.' He turns, accelerates, and we sit in silence as we speed through the suburbs.

'What's my brief?' I enquire, trying to sound respectful, aware that I know a great deal more about the ways of the world than this Matt.

'How much do you know about runners?'

'Only what everyone knows. It's a revered occupation. Counter-culture in a time of national crisis. Runners deliver. Carry traded goods, join together like-minded #isolators.'

'And you know Robin …?'

'Robin and I go back a while. We worked together on the glitch in the early days.' I lie, selective with the truth, adding, 'I was in her group when she walked back to Caernef. Picked locks for her.' I don't know how she does it, but the look of total devotion on his face is enough to make me throw up. Robin this, Robin that, like she's a god, or a guru.

'This is how it really works,' he begins. 'All you need to know is that there is a grand plan, which Robin and her advisors lead, from the folly at Caernef. The plan is based upon the runner's values: *equity and innovation.*'

I perform a three-fingered salute. 'I promise that I will do my best …'

He is offended, snapping, 'It's more grown-up than cub scouts.'

'I'm serious. I'll put everything into this.'

'Show me.'

…………

While driving, Matt grabs a folded piece of paper, handing it to me. 'We are heading here, an earth called *Superior.* It's laid out in a rough grid. We'll visit together as it's your first. You can deliver all the packets while I make the collections. I suggest you familiarise yourself with the layout before we arrive, that is, after we have made a stop for breakfast.'

I have heard about these *earths.* They are springing up across the country on common land and in farmers' fields. Host organisations rub their hands in glee at their ever-increasing bank balance, capitalising on relaxed planning laws. The residents deliberately lie low, staying off mainstream social media, so there is minimal visibility. They self-build small eco-homes. I'm looking forward to our arrival with interest.

Matt begins to lose some of his haughtiness as he describes the place to me. He clearly has an affinity with these social rebels and treats his role with extreme gravity. 'One of the rules for senior runners like me is that we stay grounded,' he explains. 'I mean, I oversee all the young runners across the region. I know each one by name, and have played a part in their training, but I still take time to deliver stuff myself. It's all part of Robin's vision for interconnected and progressive communities. You can't establish a counter-culture by replicating the very mistakes that you are trying to replace, can you?'

His question is rhetorical, but I respond, wanting to draw him out further, 'No, indeed, but the world has seen many revolutionary movements over the centuries, and look at the mess we are still in now. How is Robin's vision going to succeed where so many others have faltered?' He glances across, checking that I am genuinely interested, and seeming satisfied, continues.

'This is different. Look at the traction in only eighteen months. Surely you can see how hungry people are for change, how desperate they are for something solid and ethical to believe in?

'And the *earths*; I don't know much about them. I mean "superior" puts me off from the start. It's pretentious.'

'Ah but do you know why this earth is called "Superior"?'

'No.'

'It's Canadian, after one of the Great Lakes, because Canadian soldiers were housed in wooden shanty towns there during the second world war. After the war, through the 1950s, the camps filled with families seeking housing. You should see the old black and white photographs of the area. Now it is as if those old camps have been reborn, this time not populated by post-war homeless families, but designed and inhabited by mobilised activists, benefactors, engineers, skilled craftspeople and intellectuals. Some of them retain their second homes in British cities while living out in the sticks. It's a fascinating sociological phenomenon.'

'Blimey. I had no idea. And the runners?'

'We service their needs. We run errands. We bring supplies, we convey messages. And now, as a result of your current … misfortune, you have been catapulted into the role.'

I am grateful to Matt, and of course Caractacus, for this unique opportunity to see the #isolate communities from the inside, but I am not ready for an adventure. In need of a shower, a stale reek hangs in my hair, and there is an unhealthy slime between my toes. Even so, the sleek suit of the runner fills me with a strange optimism. Instead of giving myself a hard time over recent errors of judgement, I am empowered. I am up for it.

'You'll have to answer to Zillah.'

'What?'

'You are replacing Zillah. She left for uni. This has all happened too quickly to organise stuff for you. Anyway, maybe it is time to leave your previous identities behind.' He isn't being unkind. He doesn't seem to judge. Just practical.

'Runners stay silent on the job. It's a rule. You'll find that members of the public want to engage you in conversation, but they expect you to remain aloof. For one thing, you can't risk delays, and we also want to retain the awe and wonder. Runners are different, special, above gossip, spurning celebrity status. Oh, and you must wear the mask when in public.'

An hour from central London, the eco-car hurtles through the Hindhead Tunnel. Overhead lights blast my weary eyeballs. We shoot out into the Surrey heathland, and the motor slows. Matt pulls into a car park overlooking a magnificent hollowed-out, tree-lined landscape. Surprisingly wild. He turns to me and offers his hand. 'Welcome on board, Zillah the second.'

Despite the car park buzzing with morning tourists, and groups of walkers, it is hard to resist the majesty of the view, even for me, brought up to feel at home in city grime. 'Guess you'd like breakfast?'

Hell, would I? Breakfast. Normality. I stare gratefully into his eyes: eyes which might see more than he reveals. Following him across the tarmac towards a small café, perched on the lip of the sandy slopes, I smell pine trees. Cones rolling underfoot. Like at Caernef.

I have no money, in fact no belongings at all. The only items on me, with which I left home yesterday, are my pants and bra, now stiff with dried river water. He orders two organic vegan breakfasts, and we share a pot of tea. Unable to speak, I devour the food with impolite haste. As I pour a second cup of tea, a group of cyclists settles at the neighbouring table, excitedly acknowledging us as runners.

Matt speaks quietly, 'So, Miranda, Zillah, you're my responsibility now, and I take that seriously. Scotch any ideas of absconding, leave your worries behind you. This is a new life, embrace it and it will embrace you.'

Matt sounds like Robin.

Despite my infatuation with remaining under the radar and being self-reliant, I do believe the guy, and say so. He runs through the rules, handing me a small satchel branded with the hallowed ® of the runner. It was Zillah's. He unpacks the kit, showing me the handheld alarm, sanitiser, water tablets, painkillers, compass. I do begin to feel like a scout on safari. I never was a girl-guide. Marvelling at the low-tech, I then spot an epod, used for proof of delivery, Zillah's old phone, and there, in a special pouch, is the oke.

'You've probably never seen one of these before. It's an oke apple. We call it an *oke*. You mustn't lose it. All you have to do is to place it on your palm with your phone, and once it registers your DNA, you're trackable.' In full view of the unseeing tourists coming and going for coffee and cake, he dusts my palm with the magic of the oke, linking the phone, my hand, and the little device. It beeps. 'Oh, you've already been linked to an oke: how come?' he observes with curiosity, 'But it's been disabled.'

'Yes.'

'What's the story?'

'I know Hayden Eckley. It's now with Reginald De Vere.'

'Oh.'

'I never used it.'

'You bring all sorts of baggage to this role. Sure you can hack it?'

'Yes. I'm sure.'

'Let's get today done, and then, if you want to talk …'

'Thanks.'

While he polishes off the breakfast, I decide to freshen up. I take the runner's pouch with me, aware he will know if I plunge down into the valley below, as I am now, once again, trackable through an oke. Robin's prisoner.

Two older ladies are queuing for the toilet, words spilling out of their mouths at speed, until I arrive, when they gawp with admiration in their eyes. I silently discard the trendy baseball boots and stretch one foot at a time under the tap, sluicing off the residue of the Thames, then holding each foot in turn under the hand dryer, a public toilet ballet-dancer. I play the game, beaming beneficently at the ladies, while the roar of the dryer prevents any conversation. I scour my face, my arms, and hands, emerging on to the lip of the land glowing, the breeze catching my wet skin, while rays of autumn sunlight glance across my iridescent runner's suit. Believe me; I didn't intend to kill Jennifer Hayward. My big mistake seems to have been more serious than I originally imagined, but for now I am Zillah: Zillah the runner.

SUPERIOR

Matt takes me on the 'scenic' route to *Superior*. Our eco-car glides purposefully downhill, under the canopy of trees, a carpet of fresh leaves adding layers to years of leaf-mould. He opens the window and breathes deeply, sighing with pleasure. It smells of rot and decay to me, but I keep my counsel.

Late-morning autumn sunshine dapples the ground, teasing between the twigs of a huge canopy of trees. Matt probably enjoys the show, but its beauty hurts my eyes. Winding down and down, we are entering the bowels of the earth, it is as if we are on a journey into the heart of darkness itself. Civilisation, only half a mile behind us, has completely disappeared. Silence hangs in the earthy reek. Trust Robin's gangs to choose primeval places like this. They are not for me.

The eco-car slows, the road flattens, and before I have time to exclaim, we are driving through a ford in a flowing river, to our right a brooding lake, framed with immense trees bending down, drinking from the black water. Rusty grills and weed. What the hell am I doing out here, I ask myself? The car crests a small rise and Matt draws up, under trees. We are in a car park which might as well be underground, as despite the thinning branches above our heads there is little light. He is efficient, and does not treat me as a novice, shoving the packets and parcels from the back of the vehicle into a sack, which he launches on to my back.

'There! Let's see whether you can cut it as a real runner!'

He jests, grabbing his load, and whispering to me, 'Time to run, Zillah.' I follow in his swift footsteps. We skirt the lake on a small well-trodden path, avoiding the lumpy tree roots, then a second lake, and a third. His legs are long, and he sets an ambitious speed, which tests me, but I keep up. We stride along a bank at the end of the third lake, and then climb. Just as I am becoming bewildered by the thick peaty air and the flashes of sun from between the high branches, Matt stops, panting exultantly.

Completely unprepared for what emerges over the horizon, I freeze, unable to suppress expletives. Matt stops beside me, gazes at my face, weighing me up. 'You're impressed?'

'I had no idea.'

'And this is one of the smaller ones.'

'Fuck.'

'You ready? We must leave by midday. More drops this afternoon.'

'I'm ready.'

On the vast area of flat common, futuristic but temporary dwellings have grown out of the land. Many of them have turf rooves. All single-story, brown and green, the exteriors built with mud and hewn wood, but solid, strangely welcoming. It is as if I have travelled back to the times of the ancient Britons but that they have discovered 21st century technology. People are busy everywhere, many holding unfamiliar digital devices rather than actual phones. A crowd of children surrounds us cheering, following, as we set off on our delivery route.

First, we locate the "round house", which seems to be a communal meeting hall. I glance inside, intending to deliver the first package into the covered wicker basket by the doorway. Matt says we have to collect digital signatures on the epod before we can release deliveries. I peer in, through the dust. In the slanting sunlight, people are weaving baskets. As soon as they see me, with Matt close behind, their faces open into smiles. They simply love runners.

There doesn't seem to be anyone in charge, so I wave the epod at the nearest basket-weaver, a young woman in a wheelchair. She produces a device and swipes it over my epod, so I can release the goods. All runs smoothly. Meanwhile Matt has collected several small sacks, and we move off together.

We run on, jabbering children in our wake, collecting signatures, placing packets in baskets. Up the main street, an old concrete road flanked by more community buildings, a simple shop, a chapel with a modest iron cross on the roof. All this, hidden, highly organised yet under the radar. Far more than I imagined. Sophisticated. Sort of Amish on steroids.

Stumbling over tree roots, we reach beaten earth paths leading to half-finished dwellings. People, of all ages and a multitude of nationalities, sing, build and sit talking in the sunshine. They acknowledge our arrival with cheers, smiles, and admiring looks, but just as Matt said, they don't engage us in conversation. It is as if we are in our own bubble, passing through a dream-world.

After half an hour of deliveries, while my bag is virtually empty, Matt's has filled up. We pause, on a bank, and share out the goods he has collected, loading them on to our backs. I am left with one final package to deliver. 'Last House, Superior' is printed on the large brown envelope. But I can't see the *last house*.

I turn to the children, asking 'Last House?' and they giggle, pointing into the bushes. Following their gaze, in a small clearing, I see a cobbler repairing shoes under an awning. As I hand him the package, he waves his device across my epod, 'Great!' he says to himself, intending his words for my ears, 'There are some things we simply have to source from outside, and I need twine, as well as needles.' He tears open the packet and reels of thick brown thread fall out on to his bench, along with an old-fashioned paper wallet of large sewing needles. Something small and spherical also rolls out. He quickly secretes it in his overalls.

Maybe an oke?

It is nearly midday, and Matt is looking anxiously in my direction. Unwilling to leave this weird dream so soon, I hang back, and take one last look across the common before I jog up to him. We take off, swift as arrows, back round the three lakes and to the car park where someone has deposited crates of eggs, which Matt loads gently into the eco-car.

'Not bad,' he admits, 'You are quick, but too curious.'

'I've never seen anything like that before. Tell me more.

Matt flicks on the motor and strikes a deal. 'You tell me about Miranda, and I will tell you about the earths.'

. . . .

He's a nice guy, but I know not to trust him, so begin cautiously as we pass back through the dark jungle towards civilisation. 'Miranda worked for Reginald De Vere at De Vere Stratagems.' Pause.

'Is that all I get?'

'There's nothing interesting about Miranda, it was a cover story. She ran errands, helped to fulfil various government contracts. Miranda was put in place to stop the glitch.'

'But *Robin* managed to stop the glitch, well over a year ago now.'

'Robin stopped nothing. It came back. It continues to come back.' I am not giving anything away that is not already known to this brainwashed runner, but as I talk, I remember Rupert's small silver flash drive. I memorized the dates before handing it to Reginald. Tomorrow is the first likely glitch. Reginald knows. Rupert knows. Maybe Hayden Eckley knows. Algernon's security committee certainly knows. They will be poised right now, ready to cut the power, ready to block the signals. They are intent upon preventing Robin's rebels and dissenters from doing … from doing what exactly? Maybe Superior operates outside the tech props of society.

'Matt, there's something odd about Superior, about the earths. What is it?'

'It's probably got something to do with what you aren't telling me about De Vere. But no matter. Just don't take the earths at face value.'

An awkward silence lurks between us. Aware that I am totally dependent upon this man for the present, I know that I must give more, so, as we emerge into the real world, traffic builds, and people rush along pavements, I offer, 'Meredith Brenton is far more interesting than Miranda.'

'So, Zillah, Miranda, tell me about Meredith.'

What begins as an attempt to provide useless information masquerading as gold dust, quickly becomes a deeply personal interrogation. I had not reckoned on Matt's powers of perception. 'You tell me that you were brought up in a den of thieves and drunks, that you failed at school, but that you worked and studied. I can believe that. Getting a first in criminology isn't easy, even these days. But what of your principles. What gets you up every morning. What do you seek?'

I think, unwillingly, of the question which I so often avoid. What do I really want from life? Truth is I don't know, but I'm not admitting that to him, so I mutter, 'I love the strategy of it all.'

'So what?'

Matt begins to sound like Robin. He listens, he reflects, and then he poses the very question that you don't want to hear, but in such a devious way that he sounds so reasonable. Now he even quotes Shakespeare, 'All the world's a stage, and all the men and women merely players.'

I can finish that one off, and I interrupt his flow, 'they have their exits and their entrances.'

Matt turns towards me, the eco-car swerving very slightly, and, staring into my eyes, completes the piece, 'and one man in his time plays many parts.' Then, focussing back on the road, he adds, 'I don't think you know what you want. In fact, I don't think you know who you are.'

'Maybe. But who does these days?'

'Robin does. Robin holds to her principles. She's a role

model for all of us runners.'

'Robin is as dishonest as all mere mortals.' The moment the words come out of my mouth, I regret saying them.

'And you know that do you?'

We are going nowhere with this conversation, and I detect that his trust in me is wavering. We arrive at our second drop of the day, and he leaves me sitting seething in the car. While he is gone, I instinctively scour the vehicle for information, finding nothing but damp leaves in the footwell and sweet wrappers in the glove compartment. Forlorn and frustrated, I sit and fume, unsure of my next step, incarcerated in the clothes of a runner, with nothing to my name but trouble. I need an out.

Matt returns, shoving his epod into his bag, grinning, 'How does it feel to be left out in the cold?'

'What?'

'Maybe you are not cut out to be a runner Meredith Brenton, at least, not until you learn to trust again. The question is, what do I do with you now?'

As the day wears on, we reach a shaky compromise. I persuade him of my worth as an athlete, a bodyguard and a companion while he is so short-staffed. He lets me accompany him on the remainder of the day's drops.

We visit several more remote communities, close to civilisation, but hidden down tracks. Everywhere, the reek of mud and greenery. Each time, we are welcomed by the inhabitants who present a diverse mix of old and young, held together by a desire to exclude themselves from the mainstream. Although they don't talk to us, I overhear snippets of their conversation. Mostly they are focusing on tasks; construction, repair, an attempt at self-sufficiency bolstered by deliveries from runners, but a hint of revolutionary talk lingers in the air. These people are both angry and hopeful, desperate to take power into their own hands rather than fall victim to a society in which they feel increasingly uncomfortable.

Matt is working me hard. I run, I deliver, and I collect.

In and out of the eco-car, with little time for my own thoughts. By dusk, exhaustion is creeping into my muscles, but I don't show it. Matt is younger than me, fitter than me, but I can top anyone else's resilience … that is, except on that cursed night. The memory singes my mind, and lodges where I cannot shift it. Hunted, desperate, and in need of a plan, as the dusk rolls into the early darkness, I cling on to my final shreds of energy with increasing despair.

'Come on Zillah, buck your ideas up, we're far from finished yet.' Matt snaps.

'It's becoming difficult to see …' I say, without emotion in my voice.

'Use the torch. Anyway, we're switching to the towns for our evening shift.'

Shit: an evening shift. I need a second wind, and I say so. He's not unkind, and after we have serviced a tiny group of half a dozen eco-homes in a farmer's field, he announces that we will stop for a coffee break before the final leg.

'I don't want you seen out there, just in case. I'll get takeaways…I'll get you tea. Anything to eat?'

'What do you mean, *seen*?'

'Firstly, your photograph is still plastered everywhere. They believe you are a killer, but now they are talking about the immunity of British spies. Secondly, I might look gung-ho but I'm as cautious as I can see you are. There are eyes and ears out there, and diners are a popular haunt of extremists, intent on scuppering the work we do. Be wary.' Matt parks, and leaps out, leaving me again to my own dreaded company.

Think Meredith. How are you going to get out of this one? I picture Caractacus, naively keen, peering over the rusted girders in the barge. I picture Hayden Eckley and the novice Jade, and I reflect upon all the industrious #isolators who I have seen today. By chance, I have landed in as safe a place as any. It makes sense to stick with Matt, for now.

············

While I wait, Zillah's device vibrates. A message? For her? I grab the phone, but nothing. I fumble for the oke and hold the two together on my palm. A message pings. It's from Robin!

"Trust Matt. You are safe with us AK"

It genuinely seems to be from Robin. Very few people know about Anna Karenina. The message self-deletes once I have read it. This system they use is okay, but I have no idea why Robin is interested in me, if not to get back at Reginald De Vere. I need to respond, to indicate that I am grateful for their irrational rescue, but not over the top. In an instant I know what to do. It's a risk. I type quickly, "next glch scheduled for 2morrow AK" but cannot see how to send, and Matt is jogging across to the car, balancing drinks in a cardboard holder.

'Here you go, get this down you ready for today's final stint.' He passes me an energy bar and the tea. The waft of his coffee fills the cab and I inhale. 'I was worried earlier but you've done well today. Robin says you're destined for higher things, but …'

'Robin?'

'I heard from her just now. She tells me not to worry if you appear hostile, and to treat you well. Now, the urban drops are different. People who voluntarily self-isolate. We are their lifeline. Most of them work from home, living in a digital bubble. So, we must be quick and unobtrusive. They are lonely and like to talk, but we don't have time. Most of them subscribe to our digital service. All we must do is to deliver and scan the epod. It's quick and easy.'

My mind is focused on Robin. I have no idea how she knows I am with Matt, or what she wants with me. Hopefully I've bought her support with the gem of information about tomorrow's likely glitch.

After dark, the urban drops are indeed much easier than those at the earths. Fascinated by the range of pale characters who only answer their obscured doors because we are runners, I am so absorbed by this weird charade whereby we knock, drop, scan, and run, that time passes quickly.

As Matt drives us away from the final block of flats, he grunts, 'Oh, a confidential message has gone out on #isolate: Robin says to expect a glitch tomorrow. She always has the inside info. She knows everything. We won't let it stop us. The epods run on a completely separate system, but your phone will probably fail. Best make our arrangements now in case systems go down early.'

The adrenalin of the day leaves my body and I slump into the seat, suddenly overwhelmingly tired, worn down by the constant need to stay alert. Matt realises, 'Close your eyes if you want. We'll head for The Hatch; it's forty minutes away. Most of my south of England runners overnight there.'

I give in to my heavy eyelids and let sleep take me over, but am woken by a gentle jolt as the eco-car comes to a halt in yet another wooded car park. Confused. 'Have I been asleep long?'

Matt's calm voice, reassuring, kindly mocking, 'Sleepy head. You snored all the way. Now come on, The Hatch is one of my favourite places.'

I expect it to smell of wet foliage, another god-forsaken close-to-nature haunt of Robin's runners, but without personal choice just now, I climb out of the car, gulp the evening air, laced with woodsmoke, and set off once more, following Matt, Zillah's satchel on my back. We run in silence. My body feels as if it is made of cardboard and my pride is dented as I fall behind. Fortunately there is a harvest moon tonight, and the path under the trees is illuminated with an insipid light. I stumble. Matt turns, sees me struggling, and jogs up. 'Here,' he fumbles in his bag, and hands me a blister pack containing two tiny white pills.

'I'd rather not.'

'Rubbish.'

He stands over me while I take the pills, smiles, and sets off again. I follow, silently spitting the pills into my hand, and dropping them on the path for the morning rain to wash away. I can do this on my own.

After no more than half a mile, I catch a glimpse of lights ahead, and hear the growl of a generator. As we burst through the undergrowth into a small clearing Matt is recognised by the dozen or so runners drinking at outdoor tables. They cheer, he acknowledges them, and begins chatting. I lurk in the background, taking in the scene.

Lights shine out of the windows of the small black and white cottage, which sits in the trees. It is in an excellent state of repair, with a collection of outdoor buildings and large tents. Runners come and go, all cheerful. Camaraderie. Music is playing inside the house, singing voices rise and fall, while a cat bursts out of the open doorway, and is fondled by a group of women who are sitting round a table strewn with the remnants of supper. I can smell cooking, and woodsmoke.

A young runner comes up to me, 'Hi, who are you?'

Who am I? I am evading arrest for a murder which I don't think I committed, and I have several names. Take your pick … 'Hi, I'm Zillah the second.'

'Great. I knew Zillah. She's gone to uni. I'm Sam. Been coming to The Hatch for two years now.'

Matt rescues me, 'Hi Sam, how's things?'

'All good boss!'

'Glitch tomorrow. You ready?'

'Yes sir! Just getting to know Zillah the second here.'

'Can you show her the dorm, the showers and grab her some food? Zillah, I'll see you out here in half an hour.' Matt disappears, leaving me with this over-friendly stripling, who chatters on as he leads me inside, a sudden burst of heat from an open fire, through the strumming of guitars, up a narrow staircase. He knocks on a door labelled "Women". Wonder where trans runners go. No reply. He takes me in and shows me a top bunk, ready-made. 'This is yours.' I long to lie on it right now, but follow him back down into a small cobbled yard with outbuildings. Five painted green doors, and solar panels on the low roof. 'Here's the showers.'

'I don't have any kit. No towel, soap, no clothes,' I confess. He takes me round the back of the outhouse to another green door labelled 'Drying room'. We go in, and a wall of stuffy hot air hits us, concentrated smell of sweaty feet. I grimace. He leads me to a cupboard, where I can select supplies. Thank goodness he leaves me here, and I sink on to a pile of blankets. Shall I do a runner? I have no idea where we are. Somewhere south of London. I can collect supplies and head for a town, a railway station. No money. The thought of yet more running sends my head into a spin, so I meekly collect soap and a towel, and head for the showers. Hang the runners' suit on a hook, just out of range. Scalding water. So hot it hurts. I sluice the guilt of the day from my skin, and rub myself dry. In the absence of any clean clothes, I squeeze back into my running kit, and shiver as the cooling evening air hits my open pores.

Sam is looking out for me. He gathers me up and ushers me into the kitchen, where I can grab a bowl of hot supper, from the various half-empty saucepans bubbling on the stove. The welcome smell of hot food is tainted by the reek of matches and gas, but I dip tentatively into a pot.

'That one's vegan.' He explains. 'It's delicious. I ate earlier.' While I perch on a bench and eat supper, he rattles on about his day, the deliveries, a new camp, and of course, he mentions Robin, his eyes lighting up. 'Robin sent us a message of encouragement, "Enough is enough. Time to act". Thousands more have signed up. The voting campaign is gathering force, and, Zillah, Robin says there will be another glitch tomorrow. Better be ready. She's amazing. How does she get to know all this stuff?'

. . . .

After a decent night's sleep, I immerse myself in the second day of training with Matt. In the rain. Expecting a glitch. Last night he "signed me up" and I managed to obtain some clothes, now nicely folded on my bunk for later. I slept like a log. Runners' breakfast was hearty, crammed into the kitchen in shifts due to the rain. Strange to be one in a crowd. Now we are arriving at the first drop of the day. An urban earth for a change, an #isolate community hidden in the back streets. Matt keeps nervously checking his phone, I guess for the glitch, but it's not hit yet. Maybe I was wrong about Rupert's dates.

It masquerades as a university hall of residence, but as soon as we are in through the security, I see it is different. Not yet eight in the morning, and most residents are working at their laptops in their nightclothes, coming to their doors bleary-eyed, swiping their acceptance of parcels on my epod, often without a word. A depressing place with downcast eyes and pale faces; the computer generation of workaholics is nothing to be proud of. Until we reach the cafeteria, where I suddenly glimpse their passion for the ideals which underpin their toil. Small groups of fully-dressed campaigners, talking with animated eye contact, as they study digital maps, making notes on their devices, over tea and toast.

Matt deals with these groups while I check the remaining packets in our bags. They take his deliveries and swipe the epod, their eyes following him with adoration, but saying nothing. It occurs to me that the notion of celebrity is turned on its head. Instead of a cult of personality, there is a shared reverence for anonymity. There's something levelling about these communities which I can't quite put my finger on.

'Don't they leave the building at all?'

'No, most of them stay here 100%'

'Blimey. What are they working on?'

'This morning they are trying to get today's tasks done before the expected glitch strikes. The residents upstairs, they all have jobs in the real world. They work from home. The activists, they are focusing on …'

Suddenly the lights go out. All background buzzing is replaced by an eerie silence, broken by the insidious high-pitch wailing we now know so well as phones begin to scream. All these people face no choice but to switch off.

So, the dates on Rupert's tiny silver drive *were* to do with glitches, I'm convinced. The campaigners have been pre-warned, thanks to me alerting Robin, and they shrug their shoulders, reverting to paper, peering in the natural light which seeps through the high windows. Matt seems tense, and ushers me out, bypassing the disabled security, back into the street.

At first, a few years ago, the glitch caused panic, violence, anti-social behaviour. Even I was scared. No one knew what was happening. We had not seen it coming. These days, the public is used to it. I watch as an older man sits down on the pavement, his head in his hands, as if to say "not again". A young goth kicks a can, again and again, into the wall. The queue at the bus stop disperses. They know there will be no buses until things return to normal, as they generally do, after an hour or so, sometimes longer.

'One day it might stick again. It might be permanent.' Matt muses, unable to unlock the eco-car.

'Only if they choose to sink mankind back into darkness again.'

'What do you mean: they? Who?'

'Robin will tell you.'

'That's no answer. Come on Zillah, walk with me in the park while they switch our backup on. You never know, someone in Whitehall might even manage to undo the hack. It's happened enough times for them to work it out.'

Matt takes my arm, in an old-fashioned gesture of camaraderie, and walks with me along the pavement, no compulsion, just friendly. We enter the municipal park, night-time chains hanging loose on the iron gates. Even nature has to be locked up after dark here. Wet bushes, litter and pecking birds, which Matt identifies while I scan ahead and behind. Habitual vigilance.

'So, what will Robin tell me about the glitch then?'

'It started as a malicious cyber hack. I was in with them at the time. We had some hairbrained notion of resetting society, taking mankind back to a fairer time, dismantling the layers of capitalism in one fail swoop. But they were naïve, and Robin … well, Robin collaborated with the British government to stop the glitch. For a while they were successful, but …'

'But it came back, Miranda. The glitch came back, even though the man at the heart of the cyber terrorism had been killed.'

'And why do you think it came back, Matt?'

'Dunno. Beats me. The gangs regained control somehow?'

Just as I am deciding whether to run my theory by Matt, that it is a government ruse to subdue the renegades, and to scupper the habitual home-working which is threatening the economy, not only here in Britain, but worldwide, our epods vibrate.

'Great, we are up and running again. Blast their glitch, it won't stop the runners. Come on Zillah, we'll travel to the next drop.' Matt's schoolboy enthusiasm to resume working ends our tete a tete in the park. Perhaps helpful, as I shouldn't be confiding in him. His arm through mine is no longer an amiable gesture. He pulls, and I wince.

'But our next drop is locked in the car?'

'Just watch!' He uses the epod to override the locking mechanism, and we dive back in the car, which starts. Glitches generally scramble vehicle systems. Every time the manufacturers devise a workaround, the glitchers rework their algorithms. Our challenge now is to negotiate the stationary traffic, all normal vehicles disabled again as their digital systems are dead. Only a few expensive cars with newly installed override proceed cautiously. We swerve round the cursing populace, and avoid catching the eyes of despairing characters, caught completely unawares, yet again. Matt is used to negotiating the incapacitated streets, and he weaves through the weary mayhem. But as we approach the next urban earth, a tall block masquerading as offices, I can tell we are being followed. In an instant, Matt's usual calm turns to panic. I was half-expecting this. Sirens, blue flashing lights. Police have a glitch-override too.

Matt is shaking, 'Robin warned me of this. Miranda, take the oke. Now.' He thrusts his oke into my mouth. I gulp from my water bottle, gagging. The small sphere travels down inside me as they drag us from the vehicle. Handcuffs. Knees in my stomach as I struggle. Not even time to thank Matt, as they drag him into a separate police car. No reverence for runners here.

'We are arresting you for the murder of Jennifer Hayward.'

INSIDE

I ache all over from boredom and inactivity, sitting on the stainless-steel bench, hour after hour. Hard blue plastic cushion. This is fucking ridiculous. They won't let me see anyone, the food comes at odd times, sometimes not at all, and looks like crap. It took ages before they managed to find a lawyer. When he eventually arrived, introducing himself haughtily as "Charles Shakespeare", I could see he had already labelled me a trouble-maker and didn't believe my story. They won't tell me whether Matt has been detained. But worst of all is the doubt in my brain. Seriously, I can't remember. I didn't mean to do anything other than fire a warning shot. At the time, I wasn't aware of blood, or cries. I left the window, nearly tripped over the cat, but there was no noise behind me.

To crown it all, they say they are investigating me for terrorism offences in connection with international liaison, as well as the murder. Seems to mean they can detain me longer without charge. I'm not a terrorist. I certainly don't support the current government, but I've got no *cause* to promote. In fact, I don't know what I believe in, so how can I be a terrorist? I've learnt to slip noiselessly from one side to another depending upon my brief. This is escalating completely out of proportion.

I saw Reginald De Vere through the downstairs window, clothes off, glasses off, with a woman. I didn't even know who she was, but she seems to have been someone called Jennifer Hayward. I took a photo, then fired a warning shot. I've thought about that. It was intended to blast him into his senses. I care about him.

Then I accessed his account on my phone and posted the image as if I was him. In anger. A weakness. A mistake. That's probably a crime, but that's all.

They have taken Zillah's satchel; the few items in there will now be rolling around in their locked confiscation trays. I don't even have a watch, so try to gauge the time of day from the pathetic patch of daylight which travels across the ceiling. Oh, for a phone. Fuck; it stinks in here. Disinfectant, sweat, bodily fluids. The air is thick with it. The toilet doesn't help. Can't eat sitting next to an open toilet that's been used by a string of drunks and addicts. The clothes they forced me to wear stink too, of cheap washing powder which hasn't succeeded in removing whatever was there before. Grey joggers and a top replacing the beautiful suit of the runner, which they have confiscated as evidence. Of what? They even removed the baseball boots, replacing them with some old black plimsolls. No socks. But they're okay for exercising, which I force myself to do several times a day. Seeking a grain of sanity as I stretch and jog, on the spot of course, my body stripped of its identity. It seems to belong to someone else.

I'm continuously on camera. It bores into my skull. Wonder who is watching. And the silence drives me to distraction. Occasional distant slamming doors punctuate the boredom. At the beginning I kept jumping up, thinking they were coming for me, but I soon realised the most galling punishment is being unimportant. After the booking-in and the identity checks, there's only been the lawyer, and the food, which I ignore. No questioning. Nothing.

Don't mind being lonely. Used to that, but I'm not used to being the victim, not since I was a kid. I've been thinking of Nelson Mandela, of Aung San Suu Kyi, of Julian Assange. How did they manage? I'm at risk of going off my head after less than two days. And one face keeps invading my consciousness. Robin's face, plain and old, serious, weather-beaten. Secretive. Eyes that see through you and back again. The revered and adored Robin: my saviour, my nemesis, once my companion, and now my critic.

Robin's face, raising her eyebrows as if to say, *what are you going to do about this then?*

Okay, Robin, I'll tell you what I'm going to do about this. I will prepare my case. I will stay alert, fit and sharp. I will get myself out of here and back to a normal life if it takes all the energy in my body.

You'll need to eat then, and drink. Keep your strength up.

Robin, nagging. I turn to the flimsy plastic tray of brown stuff which was thrust in by a hairy hand on the end of an anonymous arm a few hours ago. The food might have soaked up the smell of the cell. But Robin's right. She's generally right. I stare fixedly at the patch of light on the ceiling, clench the back of my nose, and eat. Some sort of lentil bake. Meant to be eaten hot, but now flaccid and tasteless.

All of it, Miranda, eat all of it. Robin, the nagging mother I never had.

In the corner there's a water dispenser. Standard survival: water in one corner, toilet in the other. Passing through me in between. One plastic cup. Water.

Okay, what do you know? Even now, Robin is trying to extract fresh intelligence out of me. Reckon I know more than she does about the glitch, and the conspiracy surrounding it. I wrap my arms round my knees, turning my back on the toilet, feet up on the bench in a futile act of defiance.

Tell me then.

Fucking go away. Shut up and fuck off. Leave me alone. God, you don't think swallowing that oke thing has allowed her inside me? Surely not. Silence. Maybe the world has finally ended, the glitch has won, and I am the only person left, locked in this shit hole. Trapped. Hate being trapped. Smears on the walls. Wet on the floor. Patch of light on the ceiling. Time moving oh so slowly. Hour after Hour.

59

Robin?

Yes.

You still there! You sound far away.

Miranda, you were going to tell me about the glitch. You say you know more than me. Come on, spill the beans.

Deep breath. Another mistake, as the air is polluted. Contaminated. I am contaminated. Unclean food which *you* made me eat. Contaminated by guilt. Guilt for a crime I didn't commit.

The glitch, Miranda, focus. The glitch?

The glitch originated as an attack on the establishment, and it nearly succeeded. But they despatched Todd Humboldt, the mastermind, and they silenced Karl Campbell, my hero, leader of the Year Zero movement, the brains behind the vision to re-set normality into a post-capitalist utopia. The glitch succeeded in that it forced the world's population to think, to stop taking things for granted in the stunned years of post-pandemic sadness. The grip of humankind upon the earth is no longer taken for granted.

Yes? I had worked that out. That's why we set up the runners, as the earths and the #isolate communities grew in strength. They needed connectors. Young, keen super-heroes …

Hold on, I hadn't finished. You will get a turn.

The patch of light has travelled right across the ceiling and is staining the wall, soon to disappear as the automatic lights turn on. Lights that, I eventually discovered, only stay on if you move under the sensor. Abdominal pains. That foul food, or that ridiculous oke, splitting my intestines. I hug my screaming stomach. Get a grip, Miranda, once Meredith, once Zillah. Get. A. Grip.

So, the establishment won, and the worldwide glitch stopped. For a short time. But two new phenomena began to rankle, to get under the skin of the comfortable self-satisfied politicians and their chums in business. Firstly, people started opting out. Some through fear, others through a desire to take control. They turned their backs on the society which had disappointed them, and they took comfort from those close to them: friends, family, trusted colleagues. They looked back to times when humans grew their food, baked their bread and defended their borders. They refused to bury their dreams. The "earths" grew and grew, under the radar, off-grid.

They would never have taken off without the runners.

Yes, I'll give you that.

And the second thing?

You know it. Work gives people confidence, identities, purpose. But fear of the streets, fear of the very air they were breathing, sent them indoors. They grew pale, workaholics tethered to their computers, to their phones. Held together by that fragile thread called the internet. Zoom, Google Meet, Web Ex … desperate to justify their existence, to make a difference, to contribute, they voluntarily locked-in.

Again, without runners, they couldn't have succeeded.

Okay. Okay. But are you proud of these barely alive automatons? Are you proud of causing the proliferation of insipid prisoners condemned to a life of indoor, screen-dependent work? Are you?

It's not like that …

Hell it's not! Anyway, listen to this. At this crucial point, the balanced fulcrum of power and of people, at this point. Wait for it … a secret government committee took control of the glitch.

What?

I've seen evidence. They are promoting the idea that the glitch is a result of cyber terrorism, even caused by #isolate, but really, they, THEY, are controlling it to try to force the #isolators back out into society. They are scared that there is a tide turning on the economy. It's not in their interests for earths and isolators to succeed. And there's something about the forthcoming General Election which I don't yet understand. Something big and ingenious is afoot. Over to you …

Robin?

Are you there?
Silence.

. . . .

When they dragged me in, they asked whether I had a preference for my representation. On reflection, not only was this a sour joke, but my request for a disabled black woman to represent me, was unwise. I once knew the most amazing disabled black lawyer. She gained my respect from the first sentence which escaped her eloquent mouth. But here, here, I have ended up with the duty solicitor, the typical white, overweight and suited sycophantic misogynist. Charles fucking Shakespeare.

'Name?' He bellowed. That was problematic in itself. When I explained that Meredith Brenton ceased to exist, I could see him jumping to conclusions. 'Your real name?' he tried again. I shrugged. After several insulting questions, and my refusal to cooperate, he grew frustrated, enforcing a parent-child dynamic upon me, so I clammed up completely. 'I am here to represent you, Ms Brenton. It is in your interests to be open with me.' In no uncertain terms, I told him where to go, and he left, without a word. I've not seen him since.

It's dark outside and I'm beginning to hear muffled voices. The slamming of doors interrupts the silence. By my reckoning it is Friday night, and the custody cells seem to be filling up with revellers. I hear a coarse voice yelling, 'I'm warning you,' but no one comes for me. Abandoned and festering in this hell-hole, tormented by an unknown future in the grip of other people's whims. Labelled. But I'm still not sure. Griping pains. Head swimming. Robin? Are you there?

Being alone is alright as long as things are working in your favour. But the stink, the food, and hour after hour of being ignored is making me vulnerable. When I stand, fully intending to scour the walls for any opportunity to escape, in vain, like so many before me. When I stand, my legs waver, and my head swims. It's deliberate on their part, making me so desperate that I confess. But I have nothing much I can confess to. Remember Giles Corey, in *The Crucible*. At the age of eighty, he steadfastly refused to accuse his wife Martha of witchcraft, and paid the ultimate price, pressed with stones for two days until he eventually died, without betraying his wife or compromising his principles. I am under such a stone. My flesh bruised and my heart in spasm.

A key in the door. At last. No. It is in the cell next to mine. Thuds, wails. People crying out.

Under no illusions, I know I am no Giles Corey. He held out for his principles. I am just a cheap opportunist. I don't know who I am or what I want from life.

What do you want Miranda?

Robin, you're back!

So, tell me what you want?

I don't know. All I want is to be out of here. To be somewhere else. I can tell you what I don't want.

That's a start.

I don't want to be pushed around by people who think they are better than me. I don't want to be a victim. I don't want to be seen as … seen as the fraud that I am, weakly dishonest, paid to spy. Don't get me wrong: I am proud of my achievements. I simply don't want to be ignored. I don't want to play second fiddle to you, Miss goody-two-shoes, beneficence and selflessness shining out of your arse. I don't want to see the adoration in people's eyes when they say your name, and the distrust when they glance at me.

What do you believe in, Miranda?

I believe in the right not to answer your endless questions.

Zero out of ten. You can do better than that.

Alright, you win. I strive for ten out of ten. Be the best, the cleverest. Outwit them all, and come out on top.

Why?

What the fuck do you mean, why? Because. Because I had a crap start and I let myself down. Because I want to

63

prove … prove that I'm as good as anybody else. Better. Prove I am better.

Tell me about what "better" looks like.

Tougher than the best boots you can buy. Quicker than Usain Bolt. Sharper than a scalpel. I want to be able to attack a problem, find an out-of-the-box solution and enact it before anyone else has even guessed step one.

Not much then …

Don't you dare laugh at me.

I'm not laughing.

My patience is at breaking point in here. This isn't helping.

Tell me what you thought of the earths.

I was blown away by the rural ones. So many people, all ages, all types, working together, creating a real community. Even I was tempted to stay. Never seen anything like it before. And so hidden. Clever. Under the radar. They are totally dependent on the runners though. That's a weakness in the model. If you go off-grid these days, you need some sort of reliable connection, even if you are largely self-sufficient.

The city places were depressing; quite a contrast. I felt sorry for the workaholics with their drained faces and desperate eyes. Casualties of today's society, lacking vitamin D.

You felt sorry for them?

I did. I could easily imagine myself in their shoes. I can understand their desire to escape life's trials by working 24/7, but the internet is addictive. It can fill a hole that isn't there. They each seemed to be missing something.

Sunlight?

Maybe. More than sunlight. They were too insular. They looked so miserable. I wanted to drag them outside and let them loose …

In woods, fields …

Smelling of dank, wet greenery.

Better than smelling of the place you're in.

Touché. Caernef is your nirvana. It is your engine room. You have created a place where people feel at home, and where great minds seek to outwit systems. You are there, and I am here. It's simply not fair. You had advantages right from the off. I didn't. All I had was trouble, hunger, violence and failure.

Feeling sorry for yourself Miranda? Make your own luck. Prove yourself.

Fuck off. Fuck the hell off.

I climb on to the sleeping platform, and punch the security camera. Bright red blood splashes out of my knuckles, and only then does a key turn in my lock.

. . . .

A hassled policewoman pushes the door slightly open and glances in. She sees my bloody fist, frowns and disappears, re-locking me in, without a word. I feel stupid. Sit back down, wondering whether she will return.

More waiting. Voices. The grill in the door slides up. She's back, peering in anxiously, 'Do you take sugar: I've got tea?'

Such a small act is a life-saver. I attempt a smile as she enters, hands me the tea and stands over me. It is too hot to drink and I inhale the steam while she stares.

'Sorry there's been a delay. We're short-staffed and the troops have been dragged into the disturbances. It was chaos out there.'

'Oh?'

'You'll be taken for questioning in the morning. That is, if there aren't any more protests.'

I'm trying to remember if there were "protests" when I was dragged in here. Just a glitch, no protests, and I ask her. She explains that, once the glitch was sorted, there was an emergency sitting of Parliament to pass last-minute legislation against spoilt ballots and it led to massive spontaneous protests across the country. Police were drafted in everywhere, leaving the stations short of staff.

The runners were talking about this, I am sure, and I ask

65

her.

'It was the runners, the #isolators and their supporters. Came out of the woodwork. Government's met its match this time. There wasn't much violence after all, but a lot of noise. Several national journalists joined the protestors. It will be all over the papers. It was a waste of time anyway. There was no need to protest because the lawyers said the government was out of order.'

'I miss my phone.'

'Yeah: they all say that.'

'Thanks for the tea.' It is strong. In my sudden thirst, I drink it too hot and it scalds my tongue. But I don't care. There is shouting outside my door.

'Gotta go. I'm on my own tonight.' She leaves me with a blanket and some tissues to clean my bloody knuckles. I hear the key turn and am condemned to my own company once again. Something is afoot out on the streets.

Robin? What's happening? What's this about protests and spoilt ballots? No reply.

Robin?

I lie on the bench, cocooning myself in the coarse blanket, willing sleep, clenching against the incarceration, tricking my brain into compliance.

. . . .

Not even time to wash, I am dragged out of sleep by an enormous police officer, towering over me with his cartoon glare.

'You're coming with me,' he growls, snapping on handcuffs, and hauling my bewildered body out through the unlocked door.

The idiot lawyer, Mr Shakespeare, is sitting in the bare room offering a beneficent simper. I determine to keep my counsel. Certainly not going to share my innermost thoughts with this imbecile.

'Full name?'

This is where the difficulties begin. I grunt minimal responses to their machine-gun demands. When they finally ask me whether there is anything I want to add, I request my phone back, but this is not permitted; I am not allowed to contact anyone. The lawyer's bulbous eyes bore into me, the folds of skin around his neck wobbling. His suit is tight, his demeanour disinterested.

'I don't want to contact anyone. I just want to know what's going on in the world. Maybe a newspaper?'

'Ms Brenton, you are facing extremely serious charges, but you are worried about the news?'

'Yes.'

'Interview terminated. Mr Shakespeare, I suggest you spend some time with your client.'

I refuse to spend any more time with him, and am unceremoniously bundled back into the custody cell, none the wiser about their intentions for me, or about what is happening out on the streets. I've lost track of time. It seems to be midday as the cell is unusually bright.

The pale patch of light travels slowly across the ceiling, goading me. The noises in the corridor intensify.

Bellowing.

Sometimes screaming.

Exercise keeps me sane and I obediently eat any food they shove in at me. Robin's gone away, but there's a strange reassurance in the rhythm of these accursed solitary hours. Interminable waiting. Oceans of time to think about my next steps, but thought ossified by the uncertainty of my position. One thing I am sure of is my primeval desire for freedom. Once out of this disinfected hell-hole, I will never take freedom for granted again. That is, if I'm not banged up for the rest of my living days. For a crime I'm convinced I didn't commit.

Guilty of so much, but not the crime they are pinning on me. What would my motive have been? They asked me if I had a sexual relationship with Reginald De Vere, and I laughed, which angered them, so I simply said 'no'. I pictured the tall, enigmatic pillar of the establishment, who I had trusted with my life, and who had trusted me. I looked backwards into his grey eyes, subterfuge beneath his veil of geniality. I didn't care for him in that way at all. They wouldn't understand. It was his cunning, his thinking, which attracted me, cloaked in a wash of respectability. He had gathered golden hordes of intelligence over the years, and once you became a trusted co-conspirator, he was generous in sharing his wisdom. 'Yes, Reginald,' 'No, Reginald,' what should I do now, Reginald De Vere?'

Meredith?

Reginald?

Tell me what happened that night. I need to know.

You know; it's so simple. I wanted to tell you about the flash drive. I thought that "He Knows" was Rupert. I thought that I had snitched the key to stopping the glitch from his careless pocket and I wanted you to know. Honestly.

But …

I hurried under the street lights from the night bus. Saw the light shining downstairs. Thought you might be awake, peered through the gap in the curtains. What did you think you were doing with her?

Well?

Reginald? Fuck. Don't go now you're here. Reginald?

Just tell me what you did.

I saw your glasses on the side table. I didn't want to see you naked. It wasn't right. You work better with your clothes on. I was angry.

Angry?

I was angry with you. I didn't know who the woman was, but it wasn't your wife. It wasn't Cynthia, was it?

No. Why angry?

It was some woman called Jennifer Hayward, wasn't it? Who was Jennifer Hayward? Why were you with her, with your glasses off?

Why did it make you angry?

Because I didn't *know*. Maybe "He Knows" should have said "She Knows" or maybe she was just a cheap thrill. But it's not like you. Jennifer Hayward knew something. You were playing me. You thought …

It wasn't like that.

You thought you could play my game, because I was so good at it. You wanted something from her, but it went tits up. You wanted …

Meredith, it really wasn't like that.

I should know who she is … was. "Hayward." Hayward, Hayward. Tustian Hayward. He was her father. Not her husband: too old. There must be a connection between Tustian Hayward, the senior civil servant tackling the glitch, and Jennifer. Breakthrough. Reginald?

Silence

Reginald?

Hey, Merri!

What?

Merri. Need help?

Dad?

OUTSIDE

Mum's addictions were extreme. As I grew, I slid down her priorities, only knowing her as a sad victim of pressures which she was unable to contest. My Dad, on the other hand, was less chaotic and more of a schemer. He knew his limits and stayed just inside them. Proud but dishonest. From dishonest stock, not prepared to graft, but with a sense of entitlement which didn't include me. I learnt at a young age to keep below the radar, to feed his addictions, whether for drink, or stronger substances, and to ask few questions. He included my brothers in his games, but as a female, I was expected to scurry around servicing their needs. Mum couldn't. Needless to say, I exited as soon as I could legally do so.

Dad?

Merri. It's Dad.

Where are you Dad?

Somewhere you will never go. You don't need to know. Water under the bridge. Now, buck up gal. What's your plan?

I don't know.

Did you do it?

No.

Two choices then: stick it out and hope the scabby sham of a justice system protects you, or run.

Run?

You've done it before.

Not from a place like this, locked up in second-hand joggers; handcuffed in guarded corridors.

There's a first for everything. Bide your time. Weigh up

opportunities. Analyse their weaknesses. Only take a chance if you are confident of success.

And then?

'Run, run as fast as you can. You can't catch me: I'm the gingerbread man.'

Dad?

Silence.

Dad?

Loneliness again.

He's right. If I stay in here any longer, I'll go as mad as my mother. I have just got to stay alert to all possibilities. Keep on top of this.

....

Hours: tedium in stinking air. Late-night corridor noise is intensifying. Loud clanging of metal. Wish I knew what was going on out in the streets. Shouting. Stamping feet. An instant of proverbial silence. Footsteps. Key in door. My door.

Pale eyes in a pale face peer nervously in at me. No uniform.

'Hi, you a protestor? We're releasing them. You're not on my list …'

I nod, pushing my way past him into the crowded corridor where police officers are attempting to restore some order. All eyes are on a group of snarling young men. Anarchy. #Spoiler. The pale face who released me is grabbed by uniform. Don't stop to look. Proceed down the corridor with head held high. Chaos. The desk unmanned. Emergency bells start. Cell doors lock automatically. Too late for me. I'm out. Grab a jacket from its hook and sling it on. Check pocket: phone. Keys. Leave them on desk. Walk out into the damp late autumn dusk just as back-up police cars turn the corner. Head in the opposite direction.

I'm running again. Pumps on wet pavements, fleet of foot and un-pursued. Through a city centre, weaving between evening drinkers. Hood up, brain on fire as I frantically search pockets and find cash. Oh joy! Don't stop to look, rustling the bank notes in the inside pocket. Road sign points to Reading railway station. Preferrable to police station. Veer, run, scan, stop.

I'm standing in front of the massive airport-style façade, which is throbbing with revellers, drinkers, and serious travellers. I'll be pursued, no doubt about that, but the officers seemed to be focused on some other disturbance. The guy who unlocked my door appeared to have obtained keys to the custody cells. Mixed feelings. No time to think now. Acted on impulse. Seek vacant ticket machine. Carefully avoid security cameras. Hood up. How much cash? Three twenties. Won't get me far. Check fares. They may be able to hack this and track me. Less so with cash. The furthest I can go in the direction of Caernef, on a single ticket, is Ludlow. I went there once. Gourmet food and tourists. It'll do. Feed cash into the slot, grab ticket. Collect change.

Ten minutes. No phone. No watch. Keep glancing up at departure board. Hell; I've lost two days of my life. Yellow lights signalling my escape route. Scoop up a discarded daily newspaper and buy cup of tea from a machine with the change. Ensuring my face is obscured. Balance tea and ticket. Through automatic barrier to platform eight. Delectably anonymous. Adrenalin. Blending into the human traffic. Board train, scan for cameras, sit. Deliberately amongst people.

Just over an hour to Newport, I hide under my hood, drinking tea and reading the newspaper, while people come and go, first at Swindon, then Bristol. Every mile further from Reading is a mile nearer a precarious safety.

Puzzling newspaper headline, "Supreme Court declares ballot intervention unlawful." I read on, while surreptitiously checking around me, eyes on stalks. It seems that during the week that I've been locked away, the countdown to the much-postponed General Election has been troubled by a massive "#Spoiler" campaign. It must be Robin's earths. Nothing else would have the numbers, but the earths are not identified. The story tells of a mounting "antisocial" threat as a media thread encouraging spoilt ballot papers goes viral. It seems the government took fright, clinging on to a tenuous lead in the polls after their most recent campaigns to restore the faith of the frightened, in right-wing control. They tried to pass emergency legislation to prevent the inclusion of spoilt ballot papers, accusing the perpetrators of tampering with the democratic process. I wonder why a few spoilt papers would make any difference.

Another story about the earths in the middle pages, accusing China of masterminding a communist plot to attack western capitalism from within.

Train slows. Automated voice says, 'Your next station is Newport.' People grab bags, rise from seats. Need to move quickly to catch connection to Ludlow. What the hell am I doing travelling to Ludlow? A random place. Too late to change my mind. Exit the train and sidle to the platform. Train comes in. I take a seat and huddle under the hood, not revealing my fear. Oh for a runner's mask. An hour and a half in the public eye and then I can run, alone and free once more. Inconspicuous.

The minutes drag. Drinkers around me shout amiably. No ticket checks. I urge the train to travel faster. We cross back from Wales into England. Hereford. Leominster. I remain unnoticed. Rigid with anticipation, planning my next move. Eyelids drooping. "We are approaching Ludlow." Not my destination of choice, but as far as my stolen cash would take me. The automatic doors open and I follow the trail of weary people out into the air. Station deserted and office closed. We pass through to the car park where people hail taxis or stride into the distance.

Zillah the runner does what she does best. Despite hours cramped on seats and a few days in a cell, my muscles respond as I need. I sprint through the darkness, avoiding the glare of street lights, flying through the shadows. Random route through houses. Keen to leave the town behind me. Streets. Houses. People. Dogs. I slow from a jog into a brisk walk, hoping not to draw any one's attention. Out, out of the town, seeking the shelter of the fields. See, Matt, I am a runner!

Road bridge ahead, over the ring-road, and into the distant blackness. I run again. Awkward here. No pavements and sporadic traffic. I'm too dark. Vulnerable. Take to the tussocky verge and stumble. Hasten forwards. Road turns into a narrow lane. I had underestimated the intensity of the darkness now I have left the town.

I walk, my breath showing as steam in the night. In contrast to the town, it is deserted out here. Fields, trees. An occasional house. The lane climbs and as I turn to look behind, the adrenalin rushes into my veins. The magical lights of Ludlow twinkle and say, "Go on, go on Zillah. Run to freedom."

I accelerate up the hill, and along the plateau. Heaven knows where I am, but I'm truly off the beaten track. Seeking somewhere to rest, I reach a small crossroads, and veer left. Out here, my escape is palpable. I spot an open barn cowering by the side of this tiny rural lane, near a couple of properties in total darkness. I check every side as best I can, and find only grass and hedges. Enter the barn. Stale animal smells. Lying in the old straw I have no choice but to sleep.

. . . .

Glorious and radiant dawn. Sun rising through the trees. Dew and spiders' webs as I stagger blearily into the daylight. Chatter of birds. I could almost become an eco-warrior like Robin in a place like this. Perfection.

But reality bites as I realise my borrowed clothes are damp and I'm seriously hungry. Probably dehydrated. Ignoring the blistering headache, I step out on to the road and assess the beautiful random place in which I ended my dramatic escape last night.

Opposite the barn, across the lane and set back, is a tiny cottage. Perhaps once a holiday home, loved and cherished.

Today it sits forlorn, loose roof tiles, covered in cobwebs, and a large padlock on the front door. It is clearly uninhabited. I poke around, trying the doors, pushing windows, but no luck. Looks cosy inside. Return to the barn and sit on the straw to plan my next steps, but end up dozing.

Sound of a car approaching. Dive out and peer past the wooden slats of the barn just in time to watch a jeep draw in by the abandoned dwelling, and a man get out. He stands, as I did, surveying the scene, drawing breath, then unlatches the gate and disappears. Nervous. I stand still, concealed and shivering despite the early sunlight.

After what seems an age, he reappears, climbs in the car and drives off. A caretaker? No point in breaking into this little haven then. The visitor to my temporary sanctuary has reminded me of my vulnerability, and despite feeling conspicuous, I decide to explore the area more thoroughly. Very few vehicles out here. Sheep. Birds. A distant tractor. Follow the lane uphill, surprised at the stiffness in my joints. Feel crap. After only five minutes I pass another abandoned dwelling, set back from the lane. This time I am hopeful. The Virginia creeper has engulfed the substantial house, covering windows with what has to be several years' growth. The brick walls sit in a swathe of ragged red and purple leaves and small trees are poking up through an outhouse with a collapsed roof. Ancient wheelie bins stand guard, plastic cracked from sunlight. But feet have worn a path round to the back, which I follow, cautiously.

Behind the building are the remnants of a once delightful garden but the plants are totally out of control. The dried-up carcass of a pigeon, picked and abandoned, lies near the rusted frame of a garden seat. Piles of old bottles. Needles. Even out here, but old needles, covered in leaves.

Scratched on a flagstone is the characteristic ®, symbol of runners. So, runners come here now. That makes sense. I push the back door, tentatively at first. All is silent. I push harder, and it bursts open. Creeping inside, once my eyes have adjusted to the dim interior, I can discern faded comfort overlaid with blankets of dust and dead flies. One day, several years ago by my reckoning, the inhabitant must have disappeared. Covid maybe. Surely there's not a body here. I would be smelling it. I check in each room, treading carefully, disturbing as little as possible. Try the tap. Nothing. Search for a stopcock in vain, but find a wardrobe stuffed with old-lady clothes: decaying skirts, blouses and coats. A goldmine for someone still clinging on to custody joggers and a stolen warder's coat. If only I could turn the water on, I could wash. Shower even.

The thought of wearing these musty abandoned clothes is not pleasant, but preferrable to my current attire. And warmer. Others have searched here before, and have pilfered all of value to them. Pain. Stomach cramps. Head. I wander awkwardly from room to room in the hope of a breakthrough.

A stopcock under the kitchen sink, hidden by old bottles and rodent shit. Without thinking, I turn it. Horrendous gurgling in distant pipes. Expecting flooding. Bated breath. Turn the tap and brown stuff trickles out. Faster and faster. Colour gradually clearing. Nothing is clean. I wipe a cup on my custody top, fill it from the tap and drink. Not too much. Risky.

Next, I find a cracked bar of dried-up soap and wash. All over. Blessed privacy. I put on some of the least decomposed clothes in layers. Blouse over blouse topped off with a bottle-green woollen jacket; the type people once wore to church. And a complementary long green corduroy skirt. Dressed as somebody other than myself, I sink into a chair and close my eyes.

Distant voices calling, 'Miranda.'

'Zillah.'

'Meredith Brenton?'

The police woman; 'I am arresting you for …' clanking. 'I am arresting you for the murder of Reginald De Vere.' No, you're not. It wasn't Reginald. They were his glasses. It was … it was … I don't know who it was.

'Miranda, it's Robin.' No. Not her. Not Robin.

Fitful dreams are interrupted by a blast of reality. The door. I am sure I heard the door. I freeze, the heaviness of a troubled sleep hanging from my limbs. Now I can hear hushed voices.

'She should be here. She must be here. Somebody has been here.'

'Robin said to treat her well. She's special.'

'Ouch! Mind out.'

'Sorry Chief.'

The faces of two runners appear in the doorway, their bodysuits shimmering. One is taller, older. He leads the way with his torch flashing around the decaying sitting room. I am Miss Havisham. The smaller runner turns out to be a woman. They rush towards me. Bewildered, and faint for lack of food, I struggle to speak. 'I'm … I'm …'

'It's okay. We know. You're Miranda, really Meredith Brenton. We were told. Simple really. Can you show your wrists as proof?'

I pull the layers of ancient borrowed fabric up my left arm, exposing the scars on my wrist. Trust Robin to remember. I try to keep them hidden as a rule. He points the torch at me, observes the raised lines on the soft white underbelly of my arm, and nods.

'All right. We've been sent to find you.'

'But how on earth did you know where I was?'

'The oke. You swallowed the oke. Remember? By the way, Matt Wolff says "Hi."'

God, who was Matt? So many strange new people. Matt, of course, the sceptical runner who trained me up. 'Is Matt okay? Last I saw, he was being shoved in a police car, because of me.'

'He's fine.'

The woman introduces herself as Anna. All I can think of is Anna Karenina. She sits kindly beside me and unwraps a package of food: chocolate and nuts. She fetches a flask from her rucksack and pours me a steaming cup of coffee. Never drink coffee, but I don't have the heart to refuse, and actually enjoy drinking it. The instant kick is welcome, and Anna gets down to business.

'Right. We will call you Miranda out here. This is Troy, my assistant. We cover the rural hinterland north of Ludlow. We were re-routed to this place by Nathan from Robin's HQ. We use it regularly. You'll see upstairs.'

Puzzled, as I hadn't noticed stairs, I follow the sleek pair as they unlatch a hidden door, and we climb a steep staircase, emerging on a landing. They show me a small and well-organised bedroom. Two single beds. Tidy. Another room with a makeshift bunk, sleeping bag and a sink, which they assign to me. Before I can sink into the alluring bedding, they take me into the third room, and I gasp. It is set up as an office. Several computers, papers, maps. Window obscured by the leaves of the creeper outside.

'This is where you will work. Now, let's get started.'

#SPOILER

At first, I thought that it was a stroke of luck that I ended up in the runners' hideaway which they call The Creepers, but now I realise that these secret boltholes are everywhere. The scale of this thing is extensive. Twelve months of subterfuge. But it would be so much easier to simply rent high street offices.

My new job began pragmatically. I'm on the run and need protection. If I work for the runners, ultimately for Robin, I maximise my chances of short-term "freedom". However, the work has very quickly become an all-consuming passion. I am ashamed to admit it, because I have to face up to the fact that I was wrong about so many things. For now, I have become one of the pale faces who work day and night isolated in their indoor world. Like I saw in the town with Matt.

I've exchanged one type of isolation for another. Instead of the superficially antiseptic police cell I'm confined to two upstairs rooms in this dilapidated has-been home. Instead of brutality and a supercilious lawyer I have young well-intentioned oddballs for company. The shadow of my supposed crime still haunts me, but by immersing myself in my work, I fend off the daemons. Rio comes and goes. Anna and Troy come and go. Occasionally other keen runners drop by.

My favourite companion is Rio, except she hums as she works with the standard ear-buds of her generation. She's spent time at Caernef and is Eva's good friend. Of Robin's untrustworthy crowd, Eva was the one who I liked most.

When we travelled together, Eva was kind, while the others were cruel and dismissive as I tagged along, under instructions from Reginald, of course.

Rio arrived on my first day, and organised me. She soon had me plugged into the demands of the runners, digitally coordinating their movements, drops and pickups, tracking okes and rescuing mystery would-be heroes from minor scrapes. As the days rolled on, she trained me in the more subversive side of the business. Now I am able to hold my own if she isn't here. Occasionally other sparkling individuals sleep over in the other bedroom. There's water and power upstairs, but not on the ground floor. I've been told to stay up here, and despite my in-built tendency not to obey the bark of orders, I obediently remain where I can't be seen. The cost of being discovered is too great.

I asked Rio why she doesn't work from home, or why she doesn't stay over, here at the Creepers. She explained that she cares for her Mum, in a tiny bungalow. Her sister covers the day, and she is on duty there at night. No wonder her eyes are often heavy for lack of sleep. She doesn't let it get her down, or affect her work rate.

She has obviously been instructed not to ask me too many questions, which I appreciate. We have settled into a comfortable working rhythm. She leaves The Creepers at dusk, and I shift into my bedroom where the light is invisible, shining through the veil of foliage, on to the tangle of a garden. Through the evening, I continue answering runner's queries on the phone they have provided. At 10pm I am told to switch off, as there are night-watch bases elsewhere. They care for your well-being and there's plenty of perks. Each day Rio brings food left after local drops. You never know what will appear. It's always vegetarian, organic and wholesome.

So, I'm willingly dependent, incredibly busy and being strangely nurtured through this weird time.

The pace has been picking up lately, due to the forthcoming election. At first details were hidden from me, but once they realised I was going nowhere, and a quick worker, they took me into their confidence. At that point, I started to work on the more interesting tasks.

We have an encrypted database which tracks every nook and cranny of Great Britain: constituencies, voting intentions, earths and runners. Although Robin's band of eco-warriors is not actually standing in the election, they are attempting to legally shift the outcome, through campaigning, and through the #Spoiler initiative. Runners are revered. They are key to delivering the messages which are swinging the mood. It is an audacious move, but I reckon it stands a chance of success, as do the social media campaigns, which we promote when there's time. It's about coming together as a society. Naïve. Post-capitalist. Compelling stuff. Attracting loads of interest, but time will tell whether it will be enough to swing the polls sufficiently on 12th December, to shift the government.

One of my early tasks was to chase up all the #isolators who hadn't registered to vote, both urban and rural. In the final few weeks before the deadline, we managed to cajole thousands to register and to organise postal votes. Many of these people turn out to be citizens who were previously so fed up with the electoral system that they didn't bother to vote at all. Our sophisticated digital mapping can demonstrate how many spoilt #isolator ballots are needed to tip small majorities away from carefully selected incumbent MPs, particularly in the re-drawn constituencies. There is an undercurrent of protest which at last has a mouthpiece. Legitimately spoil your ballot paper and be counted. Make a difference.

This is a world which I used to know so well. There were 141 seats which were won by a majority of less than ten percent of the vote, and a whole host of constituencies with majorities less than a thousand. Helpful algorithms. Three-way marginals, boundary changes and new housing estates, all in the digital mix.

We use a private and encrypted communication system.

They say it is un-hackable, but I'm not so sure. It can certainly be successfully rebooted during glitches. I have spent hours talking to complete strangers on the phone. Typical voters say they have cast a ballot in every election, but this time, feel they have been pushed too far. They will spoil it. Momentum is growing. Others are weary of voting, time and time again, for someone who hasn't a chance of being elected. Then there are the eco-warriors, worried about climate change, and those disillusioned with the system, less about politics and more about humanity.

It's a rule of Robin's; phone people and let them talk. Listen. Gather views. Check the strategy out, and nurture them through. There are thousands of lonely people backing Robin's zany plot. They have time, and digital kit. All they need is a bandwagon.

. . . .

The first of December dawns bright and cold. Only twelve days to go now until the election, and our work is frenetic. Rio brings a blast of cold air with her up the staircase. I am huddling over the plug-in heater, wearing layer upon layer of woollies on top of the runner's suit I managed to persuade them to bring, even though I am not actually running. Yet. It's the hi-tech underwear which I value most. They should market it more widely.

She flashes a smile and plugs in, but we both know that today we are likely to experience a glitch. I had the dates on Rupert's memory stick fixed in my mind. December 1st 2024 was the final one. I tipped off Robin. She sent out an #isolate alert. She didn't reply to me, or credit me. In fact I haven't heard from her directly since I arrived here.

'Glitch could come at any time,' Rio comments, 'Better get ahead.'

I notice her chapped fingers, and hit the button on the kettle. We share a tea bag. It's one of those small runner things: "Don't use two when one will do." As she curls her fingers around the mug, she poses an unexpected question, 'Do you know anything about *Anna Karenina*?'

'I've read it. Ages ago, when I was studying and blitzed the classics. I was catching up on lost time.'

'But beyond reading it. Anything else?'

'Why do you ask?'

'Just something odd that Eva said yesterday on the phone, about Anna Karenina being wound up. She said you would know.'

'That's strange. How is Eva?' I divert her attention and we tap on our keyboards, setting up the glitch override for when, or if, it is needed. She chatters on about Eva at Caernef, the camp, the success of the vision and the call of the wild. Makes me just a little nostalgic for the place.

Eva was the first person to recognise me when I tagged along with Robin's gang heading to Caernef. She remembered my face from the papers when I had to resign as an MP. I'll never totally escape that image. Would like to replace it with another; hero rather than victim. Eva has an eye for faces, but a dizzy head. Far too nice. A loyal friend to Robin. Never had a friend like that myself.

'And what about Robin these days?' I ask curiously. Rio's eyes light up, and she says she will tell me all about Robin when we stop for our break. We focus back on the tasks in hand. The forthcoming election is generating so many offers of cooperation from interested parties, particularly small local businesses wanting to be associated with #isolate and #Spoiler. We coordinate offers of fresh hot meals, sacks of vegetables, clean second-hand clothes. We allocate runners, schedule pick-ups and deliveries. My pride in this everyday working-version of post-capitalism is growing. If only Karl could have seen. Trouble is the wily opposition from the current government. Bastards.

Suddenly all goes dark: lights off, screens blank, even out here. We, and many other hidden operators, scramble with our wind-up torches, to activate the glitch override for the runners. It's a well-practised procedure these days.

'Success! Now, you wanted to hear about Robin?'

In the knowledge that the runners can continue on the

backup, we suspend our activity, and relax.

'Last month I went on a trip to Caernef to see Eva. I had two days off. It was a bloody long way. She made me leave my phone in the locked box at the gate, so I could appreciate the place. I hadn't been before. It was all new to me. I mean, I'd been on holiday to Wales a couple of times, but …'

'But?'

'Well, Caernef is nothing like that. It's nothing like anything I've seen before. You've been there, Eva says?'

'Yes.'

'Well, you know then.'

'I was there is the very early days, before the earths. A lot has changed since then.'

'Ah. It has become more of a place for pilgrimage as well as the school camps, and of course it's the place where the plans for the runners are made. Nathan handles that side of things. He's the tech wizard behind it all. Robin couldn't do it without Nathan. Caernef is like a natural shrine for belief in the goodness in the world, a look-out point. It's the hub of something much bigger, both wild and organised, simple but complex.' I have never seen Rio so animated.

She continues, her eyes sparkling, 'Here *we* are at The Creepers, working away on the latest subversive technology, but it has all come from that place, a place where there is no technology at all. It's so clever. And do you know what: Robin wanted to see me! *The Robin* asked to see me. Eva took me out to a bench overlooking the water, where Robin was sitting. She said to me that we need the simple life to show us our priorities, and we need the technology to create an alternative to the world as we know it. She asked me loads of questions. You know Robin, don't you?'

'Yes.'

'So, you know that when she looks at you, with her sad, wise eyes, and she listens to your story, it is as if you are the most important person on the planet. She has a way of giving you time which is being lost out in the real world. It's no wonder she has had all her amazing ideas about society.'

Rio pauses, deep in thought. 'She lives such a simple life herself, showing us that we don't actually need very much. Until I heard of Robin, I used to go shopping every weekend. I had loads of stuff which I didn't need. I was polluting without realising. I am so thankful that I know Eva and I got involved with all this.'

There was a time when I would have grimaced at her blind adoration of Robin, my former foe, my erstwhile friend, but not now. In less than two years, British society has been transformed, and all because of Robin, the unassuming seeker of solitude.

'Tell me more Rio.'

'While we were sitting on the bench, a school party came out of one of the dormitories and the kids skipped down to the rocks where they were allowed to wander. It was low tide, and they spent ages scrambling over the boulders and looking in the rock pools, finding sea creatures. Then the teachers gathered them together and they set off round the headland. It was a gusty day, and I saw them return hours later, rosy-cheeked, eager to tell Robin and Eva all about their adventure. I wish I'd been able to do stuff like that. School for me was weeks on end in front of a screen. Robin's right; screens aren't healthy.'

'It's what *we* do.'

'Except when there's a glitch. But this is different, isn't it?'

'How?'

'We believe in the cause. We choose to do it. You, Miranda, could walk out of here at any time.'

'Could I?'

'Of course. There would be consequences, but you would be making your choice.' So, she knows. She knows I am stuck here because I am on the run, accused of committing murder. She knows *that*, and she turns out day after day, sitting alone with me in this remote derelict house.

'Rio, do you know why I'm here. Did Eva mention that?'

Her reply is unexpected, 'Yes! Eva says that you must be

protected because you have an important part to play. She said that you were one of the original gang and they need you in the unfolding drama. I wonder what she means.'

'I'm not sure, but no doubt all will become clear in time,' I muse.

. . . .

Trouble is, I have no more dates to give Robin. The latest glitch was the final one on the list. Intelligence gleaned from my days with Reginald is quickly becoming outdated as #Spoiler takes hold. Sinking deeper and deeper into the algorithms underpinning the success of the runners, I become increasingly impressed by the ingenuity of the system. I watch *my* runners come and go; Caractacus, my saviour, running the streets of London. I see him recruit people from the streets, dodging in and out of traffic, haunting bars and catching truants. He runs the Embankment regularly, dragging my mind back to my escape.

And Matt, with his vast network of trainee runners, coaching, cajoling, yet still managing the drops and frequenting the earths. I imagine the smell of the dank vegetation as I monitor his deliveries and collections. I hadn't been aware that we were on camera when we visited the earths, and even in the corridors of the living dead in the cities. There's a hack into all private surveillance systems so we can zoom in, in case there is trouble. I even spotted Jade on camera recently, Jade, the runner who gate-crashed my meeting with Hayden Eckley. No sign of Hayden at all.

I am learning how vicious our opponents can be on social media. We regularly intervene. It's a 24/7 activity, and there's a huge band of digital nomads signed up, across the world, who assist from beach huts, camper vans and high-rise tenements in unusual places. It's ironic that the very systems Robin hates are providing the momentum for her wildly successful movement. They all still think that the glitches are caused by cyber-terrorists determined to end the world order, and #stoptheglitch trends regularly.

Governments promote the myth, stoking the fire, creating an enemy other than themselves. Classic diversion tactics. In my new knowledge of #isolate, I am itching to get back into the real world of counter-espionage, out of this bubble of young people playing at being super-heroes. I know I'll be eternally grateful for this refuge, but to tell the truth, I'm desperate for freedom, the streets and my own space.

The glitch grinds on through the day, and as we have to minimise pressure on the backup system, Rio heads for home. I am alone in the dim confines of this odd abandoned house turned den of dissenters. Our phones hang on to the shreds of the emergency signal and I am able to talk a couple of runners through tricky situations as they attempt to continue their rounds despite jammed locks, blocked streets and a generally despairing populace.

Another message flashes. It's from Hayden Eckley. *HE Knows*. "Ring me."

We are all dancing to digital tunes, messages flying to and fro, signals and surveillance, feeds, cams and apps. I am monitoring *them*, as they are no doubt monitoring me. I swallowed the oke. Thought it might cause some sort of blockage, but I seem to have been spared that inconvenience. Deciding whether to phone Hayden, and come to the conclusion there's nothing to lose. Curious. Lonely.

He answers immediately, 'Miranda, how's it with you?'

'I'm fine thanks Hayden.' A pregnant pause. 'You said to phone?'

'I have a delivery for The Creepers. Get the coffee on.'

'Okay.'

I pile some old cushions into my bed, just in case someone comes in, pulling the covers over. Take torch, take phone, but have no weapon. Slip a broken iron gadget into the pocket of a thick coat and heave it on. Better than nothing, in the absence of a Glock. Hat. Gloves. Steal down the stairs.

The ground floor of the house is unchanged, derelict and

sad. I have been incarcerated upstairs for days, and am surprised how desperately I want to escape. Shove the back door, slide out, pushing it as quietly as possible back into the frame. Pause. Listen. This is what I was made for. The darkness, the keen air and the whiff of the unknown.

Frost on the ragged grass, and the silhouettes of sparkling bushes catching the feeble moonlight. I make my way slowly round to the lane and crouch behind the decaying bins, ears alert. As I wait, and my eyes get used to the darkness, thousands of pin-prick stars become visible in the deep purple velvet above my head. The air is bitter and still. No wonder the runners have managed to keep this place secret. I recall my journey on foot from the railway station, the damp straw and the overwhelming joy of freedom at dawn.

It is possible that Hayden has been sent to snatch me. I'm still not sure who he is working for. It is possible that he is bringing a message from Reginald De Vere. My heart misses a beat when I consider this, not because I care, but because I want to be scooped back into that predictably unpredictable world of genteel subterfuge and keen strategy.

The air trembles with silence until a distant owl calls. The romance of nature is blunted by my increasingly numb fingers. Soon I feel chilled to the bone, and begin to question whether this is a hoax. Forced to stand and move around, I stamp on the frosted grass and march up and down. My crunching feet. I'm wearing the boots of runners. Life seems determined by interminable waiting.

Distant sound of a humming eco-vehicle. Closer. Closer. Retreat behind the bins. Suddenly the glare of headlights as it sails past, catching a pair of eyes in the hedgerow opposite, as I see a fox dash into the darkness.

Walk again. Stamp. Wait. Wait. Wait.

Finally, I know it is him, as the eco-car slows after the bend in the road, and pulls into the scuff of a layby in front of the gate to The Creepers. Hayden flicks the interior light on, his face serious. I jump in, close the door with a muffled bang. Pungent after-shave, blaring music, which he turns off, slamming the car into full speed.

. . . .

Hayden has taken me a couple of miles away from The Creepers, on deserted icy lanes, up high to what seems like a mountain top. He says we are parked at a viewpoint, but with the car in darkness, all we can see is black. He ushers me out on to the grass, checks his watch and begins counting down from ten, peering anxiously into the distance. Not talking to me. What the hell is he expecting: a fiery Armageddon? Extreme vulnerability is tarnishing my pleasure in this freedom. He reaches three, two, one, and I can detect anxiety in his voice.

'Bingo!'

As if a celestial switch is nonchalantly flicked on, beneath us, a swathe of twinkling lights engulfs the dark and silent scene. What was empty space has become a vibrant illuminated landscape with ribbons of lights along the urban roads, isolated farms and hamlets.

'Hi Miranda! Thought you would like to see that moment!'

'Bloody hell.'

'Impressive?'

'You came all the way out here just to show me the switching on of the lights.'

'Yes. Well, no. I have something for you too.'

'What?'

'Let's talk first.' He places a small parcel tantalisingly close to me on the bonnet of the car, motioning for me to restrain my urge to grab it.

'You knew, Miranda, didn't you. You knew that it is *our government* which is behind the glitches?'

'Yes.'

'I hacked government intelligence. Discovered that the switch-on would be at 9pm, and wanted to test it out. Now we have proved it with our own eyes. On the dot of nine, everything was restored. By *them*. Not by a band of terrorists, and not by the #isolators, which they are saying. By *our own government*. Seeking re-election in just …'

'Ten days' time.'

'Ten days. What can we do in ten days, I wonder?'

'Hayden, I know this.'

'So, what next Miranda?'

We stand in an untrustworthy silence, both musing on the same conundrums. I decide to break the deadlock, 'Hayden, I'm holed up in a derelict house. I'm out of it. I don't know what's happening anymore.'

'Miranda, you are holed up with some of the most impressive cyber equipment around. You see everything from that derelict house. Everything.'

'Yes, but …'

'But fucking what? But what, Miranda.' He glares at me.

'I see everything but I know nothing. I don't know about Reginald. I'm completely out of touch, and Robin isn't answering me. I'm being side-lined.'

'And you are surprised? You are wanted for murder *and* for escaping custody. The runners have hidden you from the law, kept tabs on you, kept you safe. Tell me, how on earth did you manage to swap okes? I was trying to track you for days and only got Reginald. Then you appear with a new identity completely, but lead me up a blind alley. What's your game?'

I realise that Hayden is in plain clothes. No runners' suit beneath his coat this time. He obviously doesn't know the intel from the inside any more. Not my *inside* anyway. I have access to all areas, so that's why he needs to meet with me. But what has he brought with him?

Deciding on the cautious approach, I draw him in, 'Tell me about life on the streets. I'm out of touch.'

'You must see the streets on all those webcams, as you track the runners? But you will not have smelt the panic at the heart of government. On the streets there is an unprecedented tide of silver, Robin's chosen campaign colour: posters, flags, placards, massive billboards, not to mention all the digital stuff. Most of it looks more like grey, but the silver image has caught on. No more red, blue, orange, purple or even green. Silver #Spoiler, everywhere. Such a simple message, "Spoil your ballot: save the world." You must have seen the up-to-date stats. It's overwhelming on the streets.'

'Yes. I'd like to be out there, to breathe it, rather than see it second-hand. Where do you stand on all of this, personally Hayden?'

'You know we're not meant to answer questions like that, but for the record, I've changed my views since our early days with De Vere Stratagems. Spending months actually working for Robin … I mean … I'm a convert. How did you find slipping into the suit of the runner?'

'Apart from a spell in a stinking custody cell, I was … am now … bloody impressed. Hayden, you know me. I'm no tree-hugger. I was brought up on the city streets, and that is where I am at home, but there is something compelling about Caernef. The rate at which powerful people, with influence, are jumping on board means that there is amazing resource, both digital influence and financial backing for Robin's post-capitalist vision.'

'Shall I update you on De Vere?'

'Thought you'd never get to it.'

'Hang on, I'm on your side here.'

'Sorry, just spit it out. Reginald hates me for what I am supposed to have done. I am the spy who is out in the cold. Condemned.'

'No.'

'No?'

'No, Miranda. You're wrong about that. You're not often wrong. Maybe you are too emotionally tied into this.'

'I don't think so.'

'Don't you want to know how Reginald is?'

'I do, out of curiosity. No more.'

'Ha! He said the same about you.'

'When did you last see him Hayden?'

'Yesterday. I want to tell you about it, because I don't know anybody else who would understand, except Robin, and she is handling her own issues at the moment.'

'Robin? Issues?'

'Forget I said that. Now, Reginald. Yesterday I returned to De Vere Stratagems for a routine pickup. He's missing *you*, and I've had to take on a wider brief. You can imagine: government panic, cracks appearing, people willing to pay for intelligence. I stood in Hyde Park by the bench, you know the one?'

'Yes. Hayden, I know. Go on.'

'I looked up at the grand old building, and the windows of De Vere were odd. My second sense told me to be on my guard.'

'Odd?'

'Just odd; curtains hanging off the rails. Not Reginald's usual tidy domain. There was no security on the entrance. I just walked straight up the stairs, which were strewn with loose papers. Torn fragments. My heart was beating faster by then, and I hurried past reception, which was unattended, into his room. Reginald was there.'

'He was there!'

'Yes, but he was in a terrible state Miranda. He didn't want me to see him. He tried to cover up, his suit dirty and his hair uncombed, and he said … I can remember his actual words.'

'Yes?'

'He said, "He knows. She knows. Now, nobody knows." I drew out a chair, and sat, as usual, at the table, trying to restore some normality. I asked who "he" was, and he simply pointed to the empty folder strewn on the carpet in the debris from … whatever … with my initials on the spine. I asked whether "she" was Robin and he turned to me with disdain. "She" wasn't Robin, "she" was you.

'It was then that I noticed his books had been rifled. All those legal journals and ancient tomes, trashed. "I'll get it tidied," he mumbled. And he went to the safe, which had survived whatever had happened. He obscured my view, the back of his jacket covered in dirt, and he opened it. He pulled out this parcel and told me to get it to you as soon as possible.'

'To me?'

'Yes. I don't want whatever it is. It's above my pay grade. I'm only the messenger. You, Miranda, are the change-maker. I wanted to help the old buffer; I felt sorry for him. I managed to track you down by pulling a few favours from runners. You're no longer trackable through the oke. Yours showed up in a sewerage plant a day or two after you were imprisoned. Would you like it back?'

'Have you got it then?'

'No way! But I have a replacement.' Hayden fumbles in his pocket and hands me an oke. I hold it in the moonlight, marvelling at the technology that allowed me to swallow one, be tracked, jettison it accidentally through my digestive system, and be re-connected. Surveillance culture in extremis.

'Hayden, thank you for doing this. I do appreciate it. What next!'

'I'm under instruction to deposit you back at The Creepers where you will open Reginald's parcel. Alone.'

We get back into the car. Downhill on the ice is hairy, and I am relieved to see the dark shadow of The Creepers. Hayden urges me not to trust the phones, and to remember Reginald's rules, even now. Stay safe. Stay off the systems. I nod, and thank him again.

THE LETHAL MACHINE

In my haste to leave, I forgot to switch off the light in the office which overlooks the lane. Another mistake. Now the power is back on, from the road, I can see a pale glow through the leaves. A giveaway. But the building is quiet, and hopefully the clue to our occupation was unnoticed. I hurry up the dusty stairs, turning off the offending light, checking for messages and finally reaching my lair. I place the parcel on my bed.

My phone is detecting subversive digital signals, just like in Oxford. I could feel it vibrating when I was out with Hayden. Nervous, I hold the phone over the parcel, but it is dead. I pause. What's going on Miranda? Count to twenty. Stretch. Relax. Reflect.

'Of course: it's the oke. I need to reunite it with the phone. I retrieve the oke, place it on my palm, and link it to my phone, which buzzes contentedly. No swallowing this time.

I can guess what the parcel contains, but I don't know why, or what is expected of me. I sniff the brown paper and catch a reassuring hint of De Vere Stratagems, turning it respectfully over and over, feeling for triggers. I wouldn't put it past Reginald to seek revenge in cold blood. It doesn't feel like an explosive device, but then Reginald is far too clever to give that away. Picturing his furrowed face, I try to envisage him as Hayden described, a beaten man, covered in dust, sitting amid the debris of a catastrophic raid on De Vere Stratagems, but I can't. He is always in control, phlegmatic, acerbic, never beaten.

Gingerly I begin to peel away the kraft paper, and glimpse the familiar burgundy … shit! A seriously loud banging downstairs. Switch off my light, silently throw the emergency lock across the door to the stairs. Strain my ears. Stand like a statue. Silence. Wait. Always waiting.

Holy Shit. A spine-chilling yowl. And again. My blood running cold, I place the parcel under my pillow and proceed along the landing, stealthily unblock the door, and creep on to the top stair.

A rush of air, as a black animal bounds past me, several steps at a time, and into the decaying lounge. A cat. It has to be a cat. I must have carelessly let it in earlier. There are rats and mice downstairs, so I am not surprised. It is probably hunting. I am bedevilled by cats these days. On that critical night, the cat …

The cat is more frightened than I was, and eagerly scrams when I open the back door. Bitterly cold outside. Spooked, I secure the door and return to my booty.

With trembling fingers, I pull the paper off the book, revealing the "A". I extract the tome, caressing the cover, thrilled, nervous and curious. On the flyleaf, in a decisively confident hand, is written, "Dear Miranda, I thought that you would like this for posterity. Life has moved on. Take care, RDV." Below this inscription is "Bg20." An alluring blend of the old-fashioned and the pre-digital. Typical.

Sighing with uncharacteristic emotion, I hope that this signifies forgiveness. It tells me that, despite all, he values my contribution. I was special to him. Or it means that he doesn't know the full truth of my actions. These doubts are answered as I gently turn the pages to locate chapter nineteen; it was one of our private habits for secret messaging. From "Bg20" I can deduce the code is one before ie "Ch19". A sentence is circled in a loop of red ink, "I could forgive it, and forgive it as though it had never been, never been at all." Relieved to be alone, as a solitary tear threatens to escape my eye. Blink it away. Stupid weakness.

Unable to sleep, I leaf through hundreds of pages bearing tiny scribbles and diagrams, each reviving memories of the plots, plans and subterfuge which we shared over several years,

The first entry, when he picked me up off the floor in Westminster, and grilled me on a bench in Regents Park. He needed someone to join a guerrilla movement in Afghanistan. Suited me well as they wouldn't recognise my face out there. I was green, but quick to learn. The training out in the Brecon Beacons changed me forever. Thought I was tough enough before that. Each time he pulled me back, I sat at the polished table in De Vere Stratagems and he fetched the latest cryptic notes from the folds of Anna Karenina. He always caressed the pages of the book, and pushed his glasses down his nose so he could print the tiny words between the printed text. Never thought I would see the pages again.

The final pages of the book bear the records of his most recent plotting. I catch the initials JH. Jennifer Hayward no doubt, and scribbled maps, *CW*. Somewhere called Wumu Zhong, and a question: *who knows now?* I drift into sleep thinking that I have missed something.

Up early. Lots to do. Stick the screen on before completing morning hygiene routine, and pause as a headline catches my eye, "Government fears cyber-terrorists will sabotage election." The article draws attention to the recent "serious glitch" and hams up the risks of cyber-attacks on election day. They are going to try to strengthen the law against interference in the democratic process. Beneath this item is an article about the growing strength of #Spoiler, speculating about the hundreds of thousands of spoilt ballots probably already in the postal system, piling up ready to offset election-day votes. It seems to me that our calculations might even be an under-estimate. I foresee "Election Day Mayhem" headlines in ten days' time.

Rio arrives. We work flat-out all morning. Time rushes by. She has brought me sandwiches, which I'm eating between bursts on the keyboard. Worried about Caractacus. He's showing up on a red alert and we can't get a view. I think that he's got tangled up in an anti-runner protest. Keep tabs on him. Signal fades, then re-appears. Decide to phone him.

'Caractacus. It's Miranda. You okay?'

'Can't talk.' He whispers.

'You need help?'

'Yes. I'm cornered.'

We try desperately to pick up any surveillance cameras in the vicinity and succeed in getting a blurry black and white live-feed on the screen. Expecting gangsters, we see men in suits, standing menacingly, covering all exits from a down-at-heel shopping arcade. No sign of Caractacus. We scour the image. The men are clearly disguising their intent, and are surreptitiously armed. This is not unusual. The camera swings automatically, and I catch a glimpse of an unmistakable crouching silhouette. Instantly imagine myself in his shoes. Weigh up options.

'Caractacus. Can you hear me?'

'Yes.'

'Behind you is a doorway. When I say "now" you will stand up. A group of five ordinary guys is coming round the corner. You can't see them yet. When I say, join the group. Act as if you know them. Tag along until you are out of danger.'

'Right.'

'Nearly … now!'

We watch the figure obey, stand, join the protection of the passers-by. We watch the suited security guards scan the arcade, but they fail to notice Caractacus. Hearts in our mouths, we see the trapped runner accepted into the group, heads bobbing. Casual. Progress. Out of view.

'Rio we must find another camera. Just in case. He may still need us.'

Rio scans again and again. No images. Only the original with the standing suits. I curse. Caractacus may be walking straight into a trap, and I am responsible. Neither of us speaks. We often assist runners, but this one is serious. Added to that, I owe Caractacus my life, at least, my freedom, and can't afford to screw up. We scan and re-scan, but are forced to wait.

'Caractacus?' No response. Five long minutes.

'Caractacus?'

'Thanks. On my way now. Heading back to base. That was a close one.'

Sigh of relief. Rio's admiring eyes. At least I've done some good today. Feels like I'm on a computer game. *Nothing is true everything is permitted.*

. . . .

Only ten days to go, and campaigning is getting dirty. There's surveillance of surveillance. Everything digital is insecure. There was a time when I would have cheered at the disparaging comments about runners, being blasted by bots on social media. Not now. Maybe I am going native like Hayden.

The establishment doesn't know what to do or where to turn. An eloquent tide of grassroots common sense is flooding across the land, with all manner of consequences. The break-up of the four nations of the United Kingdom seems inevitable as the independence brigades liaised with Robin from the start. Earths are getting publicity, pro and anti, which goes against the desire of their inhabitants for privacy and isolation. Runners are quickly becoming a symbol for the future for the younger generation, despite the relentless attacks by a cynical affluent middle-aged contingent. The government is on the run, and the opposition is either chaotically divided or has turned silver.

Wish I was the revered author of a current socio-political theory, a well-paid pollster or a celebrity sage. But the stark reality is that I'm on the run for a murder that I know I didn't commit, and for breaking custody. I'm wanted. Hated. Stuck in a damp and derelict house masterminding the petty computer game-reality of runners and isolators.

I'm up a blind alley, just like Caractacus, but who will talk me through my escape? No one wants me on their side. No one is on mine. Rio's just being polite. It all feels dirty.

The runners tend to be young and physically fit, though there are exceptions. Their ethos is health, fresh air and lean strength. Hitler Youth. No, that was out of order because Robin's vision is explicitly inclusive, empowering, and beneficent. The invisible operators, like Rio, are mentally fit: coders, cyber-experts, campaigners. Mostly youngsters who couldn't run to save their lives. Nathan's recruitment is shrewdly planned. As usual, I dodge in and out, too hard-bitten to play ball for long.

They claim that Robin is responsible for turning round the physical and mental health of a whole generation, as well as solving the youth unemployment problem. Soon they will claim that she is responsible for the biggest electoral plot of the century. Who needs gunpowder when you have okes!

It's not a time to be flippant. I can't get over the thought that this is all a game, a game which has rocketed out of control. I'm out of control. Reginald is out of control. Maybe that's the allure of Robin's vision; people's lives are out of control and they are desperate to be part of something forward-looking, something definite, a legitimate form of subversion. Dangerous, but ultimately safe.

One thing I am sure about is that it is time for me to move. I'm willing to take the risk. Leafing through *Anna Karenina* last night, it became clear to me. I must get to Robin. She's even deeper into this than I am. And the days are ticking down. Make or break. I need to be at the heart of power, not in a midland backwater.

The question is, who do I trust to get me there. No one. No one at all. Need to go alone.

Rio interrupts my train of thought, 'Miranda, Eva says that Robin wants to see you again.'

'Oh.'

'She said that someone called Gid could divert out here on his way back to Caernef.'

'Gid?'

'Eva said that you know him.'

'I know Gid alright. He and I never saw eye to eye. He's Robin's rottweiler.'

'Oh.' Rio sounds disappointed. She seems to want to assist my reunion with the revered Robin, and as it could be a very convenient next step for me, I ask her to set it up, but only if I can be spared from the work here. Despite it being an incredibly busy countdown to 12th December, plenty of volunteers are coming forward at the moment. Rio promises to find out more about the possibility of Gid's transport.

Gid is an enormous bully of a man. Roughly spoken and with coarse habits. He made it his business to suspect me of subterfuge, to insult me, constantly seeking to prove his physical prowess over mine. I trusted Gid even less than I trust the man in the street. I don't want to rely on him to get to Caernef, but needs must. There is a magnetic force pulling me there. I don't understand why, but the time is right.

....

He's late. He was meant to be here at eight. The rain is beating on the creepers and there is no moonlight. Rio left for home a couple of hours ago and I have been waiting, alone and tense. I only have Rio's word. Deliberately no digital messages. I have double-wrapped *Anna Karenina* in waterproof bags, and am dressed as a runner, because it fills my limbs with a sinuous power, and raises my spirits. But Gid is late.

Maybe he won't come, and I will have to greet Rio with embarrassment, the morning after our moving farewell. Hate dependency. Hate Gid. But my choices are severely limited at the moment. Sitting in the dark window, peering out into the night, planning what I will say to the man who bristles every time he gets near me. Hoping this isn't yet another mistake.

A single headlight on the lane. Diagonal sheets of rain.

The characteristic roar of a motorbike, an aggressive twist on the throttle, before he switches off, and swings his leg over. I was expecting a car. He is jet black from head to toe, and I can hardly see his giant form stand, clad in armour and helmet, steaming. He lights a cigarette.

I descend the stairs in a daze, creeping out of the back door, maybe for the last time. Smell acrid exhaust and hear his boots on the gravel.

'Gid?'

'Ssh'

'Hi.' I whisper.

'Miranda,' he growls.

We stand so close that the smoke from his cigarette lingers in my hair, and we size each other up.

'Didn't think I'd see *you* again,' he hisses.

I cannot bring myself to thank him for coming out to this god-forsaken spot to collect me, so I simply say, 'Ready if you are.'

'You don't look ready to me,' he mocks, opening one of the panniers and dragging a set of leathers out into the rain. 'Here.'

I place the precious *Anna Karenina* in the pannier and he clicks it shut.

In silence, he watches me remove my boots, slide awkwardly into the leather trousers, clumsily balancing on one foot to re-lace a boot, while my sock soaks up water from the puddles. Boots on, he helps me with the jacket, zipping me in with a leer. He places the helmet on my head and tucks my hair into the collar with an unexpected tenderness.

'Thank you.'

'You're welcome. It's a couple of hours on the bike. Any problems shout. You must hold on tight, both arms, all the time.'

'I have ridden pillion before. I'll be fine.'

He grunts, fastens his helmet, and mounts the bike, signalling to me to climb on behind him. Secretly terrified, my adrenalin high, I cling to his wall of a back. The engine growls. He spins the wheels, for my benefit I'm sure, and we tear down the hill towards Wales, leaving The Creepers to become a distant memory.

. . . .

As a young child, I always wanted to ride on the highest roller coaster, the fastest waltzer and the tallest, wildest wheel, but our family didn't do that sort of thing, so I made up for it as a teenager, working my way to free rides. Once let loose, I won impossible dares. But this ride, clamped to Gid's back, is surpassing all those mad adolescent thrills.

Mile after mile, clinging on to the backbone of the furious machine. Legs gripping, tensing every single muscle in my body. The engine's roar reverberating in my helmet, mixing with tyres on wet road, ears ringing, head throbbing. Grinning inanely for nobody to see. My eyes alternating between tightly shut and stretched open.

I'm even vicariously enjoying being totally at the mercy of another person's expertise in handling a potentially lethal machine. Dicing with death on every corner as Gid brakes late. He's showing off.

After an hour the rain eases, but the road is still wet. Gid shouts that he wants to stop. We swerve into a rough layby, both pulsating with the reverberations of the journey. He switches off, ignores me, and I hear his fumbling fingers, followed by a gushing sound as he pees into the wind.

'We'll take a quick break. It's quiet enough here.' We remove our helmets, and as he sits on his, I follow suit. He lights up, without offering one to me.

'Quiet enough for what?'

'I've been told to keep you well-hidden. Perhaps you'd like to tell me why.'

'You must know.'

'I know they want you for the murder of a young woman: the daughter of the sleazy bureaucrat who helped Robin to stop the glitch.'

'Thing is Gid, the glitch didn't stop, did it?'

'Why her, Miranda? Doesn't make sense.'

I clam up, the stubborn silence between us shatters any feelings of wild companionship. It's awkward. He tries again, his voice tinged with irony, 'So what's in my pannier? Present for Robin?'

A gust of wind catches us. He grabs the bike, but it stands solid. I think that he is going to set off again, but he changes his mind, turning to me, and saying, 'Let bygones be bygones.'

'What do you mean?'

'I was harsh to you before. It was out of order.'

'Is that an apology?'

'I suppose so, but only if it's reciprocated.'

My words hang quietly inside my head, waiting. Despite the darkness, I can pick out the whites of his eyes. 'I trust no one.'

'Have it your own way then.' He gets up.

'No. Hold on. Hear me out Gid. I don't really know you at all. The first time I saw you, I watched you swinging the axe on the firewood back at The Pike. You didn't see me. I thought, *there's a guy with some repressed anger.* Then I watched you, hour after hour during our trek to Caernef with Robin, Eva and Nathan. Your loyalty to Robin, your determination to somehow beat the system with your fist as well as the mass of your determination. I didn't need you to like me then, and I don't now. I was Robin's unwelcome gate-crasher. I was working for Reginald De Vere.'

'So?'

'Okay, I'm sorry if I offended you back then. Let's put it behind us.'

'And the murder?'

'Surely you know I didn't do it.'

'I know that you can lie convincingly, Miranda.'

'I wouldn't have had a motive.'

'You tangle with those at the top of the country. This has something to do with that De Vere bloke.'

'Of course it does. I caught him with his trousers down.

But I didn't kill her.'

'Hold on, there was nothing in the news about that.'

'What do you mean?'

'The tabloids would have had a field day, but all we were told was that a *lower tier* spy had taken revenge on … what was the guy's name … Sir Tustian.'

'Really?'

'Yes.'

'But that's not right. I was stuck in the police cells for days. Didn't see any news.'

'So you are telling me that the woman was Reginald's lay.'

'Yes.'

'Think there might have been a cover-up here.'

'Gid, I am not proud of one thing. That night I took a photo of them together. Virtually naked. You know. And I posted it on Reginald's social media with the caption, "How to solve the glitch." I was stupid. I fired a warning shot. Only one, but not at her. I remember now; I aimed at the tree-trunk by the window. I wanted to blast him out of it. Stupid man.'

Gid laughs, a long, low, throaty laugh. 'You were lucky not to be hit with your own ricochet. They soon hushed all that up. Meredith Brenton, I knew you were canny. I knew you had it in you, and it's good to know I don't have a cold-blooded murderer at my back. Now come on, let's get moving.'

He lifts my helmet, adding, 'Robin's not well. Be kind to her won't you,' as he places it gently on my head.

CAERNEF

By ten o'clock Gid is spinning the wheels on the gravel of the familiar driveway to Caernef Camp, past guards, lookouts and barriers. Things have changed here. He parks up. Even I secretly marvel at the cosy lights shining from the dormitories, and the dying embers of a bonfire surrounded by empty log-seats on the parade ground.

'Great ride. Thanks.'

'You're welcome.' I start at the gruffness of his voice, but he winks at me, helmet off, and retrieves *Anna Karenina*.

Unsure what my next steps should be, I take the parcel and hang back, expectantly. 'They will all be waiting to see you in the cottage, with Maria and Thomas. Better prepare your speech.'

'Speech?'

He grins, and tells me that, as I am expected, they will want to hear about my values. He leads me down towards the cottage, explaining that I mustn't spend time in the camp as I haven't been checked. They are keeping the school visits as separate as possible from Robin's campaigns. Left to wonder whether he is being ironic about the speech, I consider what I might say, aware that values are not my strongest point. Looking forward to confronting Robin again. She's the one with the values: *equity and innovation*. Apart from the time she saw me hurrying away after that terrible night, I haven't seen her properly since the incredible success of the runners and the earths, and I must compliment her. Get started on the right foot.

I've been abandoned by Gid not far from that accursed

ditch where I hid during the runner event, in a tussocky no-man's-land between the camp and the cottage. Waiting again. Nerves worn by the prolonged exhilaration of the ride and brain on edge due to lack of control. I shiver, running through the few certainties in my mind: less than ten days until the election; #Spoiler very popular; hundreds of thousands of spoilt ballots already in the post; successful digital coordination of a network of runners and earths across Britain. And on the other hand, a government with the power to suspend all digital services at the flick of a switch; dishonestly pinning the glitch on #isolate's cyber-terrorism.

As for values, I'm not the person to ask, with my duplicity, dishonesty and game-playing. But since I was last here, skulking, I have changed my opinion of Caernef. I'm almost embarrassed to admit that it's oddly like coming home. But I have never truly had a permanent place to call home, and so I fight this strange feeling.

Gid emerges from the front door of the cottage and strides confidently up to me. 'I told them you've reformed. Now, it's not my place to say, but Miranda, you are going into a group of friends. Try to cut the aggression. They need you. You'll see.'

Intrigued, I follow him through the chill darkness to the glowing light. As we enter the tiny cottage, packed with rosy-cheeked people, their eyes reflecting the roaring fire, they cheer. They cheer and clap. I place *Anna Karenina* quietly on a low table, and look round for Robin, but she isn't here. One by one they come forwards, slap me on the back, shake my hand. Overwhelming. Once the rumpus has calmed, they offer me food and drink, which I politely refuse in my confusion, and am rescued by a stunning woman who I do not know. She is heavily pregnant, and when she holds her hand out to me, she conveys a glowing confidence, 'Welcome, Miranda, to our home. We haven't met. I'm Maria. You will remember Thomas, my husband, although those troubled times are well behind us.'

She sounds American, but now I do remember. She is the Syrian. This is the mother of Poppy, the child whose name provided the clue to stop the glitch. She escaped from Syria with Thomas and was scooped up by the beneficent Robin.

Maria draws me to one side, 'Now, I know you would like a cup of tea?' she drawls, her dark eyes dancing, and she disappears into the tiny kitchen. Arms are pulling me, loud laughs and more cheers, as they settle me on a stool beside the roaring fire. I take the steaming mug from Maria and the room settles.

'Where's Robin?' I ask, and for a moment, a troubled silence hangs in the hot air of the small room. They do not give me an answer.

'That's why we need you.'

I want to be part of this cosy gathering. I am touched by their trusting welcome, and their open faces. But something in my character, screwed and twisted deep down, prompts me into my steely response: 'I have come here to see Robin.'

Again, an awkward silence. Not one of them takes charge. No one explains to me what is going on. Eva, squashed in the corner, is smiling, willing me on. Nathan, looking older, catches my eye, keenly. Gid radiates a silent approval. Thomas is wary, despite Maria's warm welcome, and the manager of the school camp, Glyn, stands back with Thomas. At least I can remember their names. I try hard to stop myself thinking back to the time when I was in conflict with them, here at Caernef, in the dormitory. Instead, I think of Robin's event only a few weeks ago, the haunting riff of guitar, the glittering runners and the child collecting beer bottles.

Time to play their game. Time to reward their welcome. 'And how is Poppy?' I ask Maria, adding, 'Soon to have a little brother or sister?'

It is Thomas who replies, 'A brother,' he beams, 'Poppy is a treasure. I'm surprised we haven't woken her …'

They are each waiting for me to take charge, their faces

expectant. Time to ignore tiredness and to perform.

'It's good to be back here at Caernef at such an exciting time. Only ten days to go, and we could be seeing an unprecedented, and legal, hijacking of British politics. All because of you. All down to Robin.'

They want more. Eager eyes turned upon me. 'I have been to the earths, seen these extraordinary new and resilient communities with my own eyes. I have travelled with the runners, on foot, delivering, collecting, providing the coordination which the earths need to survive. And I have played my part in the digital mastery.' I glance at Nathan. 'I have switched into glitch-back-up and I have saved the lives of runners who have been confronted by government-sponsored vigilantes. I have managed the drops and … I have even swallowed an oke.'

They laugh, and cheer again. But I am compelled to turn to the matter which must not become an elephant in this room, 'But, friends, I am wanted by the law. I will be forever grateful to the runner called Caractacus who rescued me from a rusty barge on the Thames. I do not come to you today with a squeaky-clean character like Robin. You are not looking at a saint. You are looking at a born schemer who sometimes makes mistakes … I am starting to understand the revolution which you are quietly managing from Caernef, but if you are serious about inviting me in, you must know what you are taking on. Robin is angry at the injustices of society today. She supports those who have fallen on hard times, and she befriends mavericks, thinkers, and rebels. I don't befriend anybody. I'm a selfish survivor, devious, undercover and ruthless. I'm being pursued by the police. You might be better looking elsewhere for a temporary leader.'

Think I've understood their motives. Think I've seemed honest. Await a response.

It's Glyn, the ageing Welsh hippy, who steps up, 'Welcome back to Caernef Miranda. You must help us. We desperately need someone who *is* ruthless, who can see the big picture.'

'You need Robin.'

'We already have Robin, but we also need you.'

It is obvious that they are not intending to tell me what has happened to Robin, at least, not now, in company. I can see I will need to pick them off one by one.

Nathan looks as if he has been itching to speak for a while, and I turn to him now, 'Nathan, I have used your ground-breaking systems as a runner, as a coordinator, and as a human being needing help.' I hold up my tiny oke, 'this little beauty has saved my life more than once.'

Nathan blushes, gathers his confidence, and asks, 'We need to know what's going on with the glitches Miranda. You know, don't you?'

Time for more honesty, 'I was working for Reginald De Vere and spent the best part of a year investigating the glitch, but it was only recently that I understood exactly what is happening.' Nathan seems to hold his breath. An expectant silence. They all want to know. 'The government is secretly creating glitches in an attempt to disrupt the #isolators. They are blaming cyber-terrorists to deflect attention, and in an attempt to discredit you.' I give them a minute to process this, and am not disappointed by their reaction as they burst into angry conversation.

'Miranda, are you sure?'

'Yes, I am sure.'

'How *can* we stop the glitch then?'

'I thought that Reginald knew, but …' my voice trails off. I am still confused and … feeling guilty. Give myself a hard time. Shouldn't have lost my ally and co-conspirator. I glance at *Anna Karenina*, wrapped up on the table, and remember the words in chapter nineteen, "I forgive it, as though it had never been." Gather resolve.

'Reginald knows more of the detail. Do you *want* to stop the glitch?'

'Yes!' They chorus, all talking simultaneously. They want to turn the tide in the election without any complications of glitches. They are weary of battling them, and want to be able to say that they have moved on. We talk some more, drinks are handed round, and the fire is stoked with logs. When Thomas and Glyn pick up guitars, I look beseechingly at Gid, who seems to be my guardian at the moment. He nods towards the door and I bid them goodnight, saying that I look forward to seeing them in the morning but I am most definitely not interested in digging gardens, sweeping leaves or trekking along rural paths. The atmosphere is positive. Heaven knows why. Maybe they simply have no idea what they have taken on in welcoming me back inside the fence.

....

Gid leads me, in silence, down the path to the folly. I carry *Anna Karenina*. Wet grass, branches cracking in the wind, and molehills on the narrow path. Darkness until we see a flickering light in the window of Robin's lookout, up high in the bizarre tower which guards the estuary far below. My heart misses a beat as I realise there is no escaping a reunion with Robin this time. There are so many questions which I want to ask her.

Gid turns the key in the lock and we huddle in the cramped downstairs room.

'You'll have to sleep upstairs in Robin's bunk. There's no room in the cottage, and the dormitories are a no-go area for you at present. It's comfy. I can vouch for that. Use anything you need from the kitchen and the bathroom. I'll be back to collect you in the morning.'

'And Robin?'

'Best not to ask.'

'Gid, the whole campaign hinges on Robin. There are millions of people out there hanging on her every word. People have pictures of this folly on their walls with motivational slogans. We need Robin. Where is she?'

Unable to understand the sadness in his eyes, I hear his words, 'Miranda, it's no use asking just now. Get some sleep and we will talk more tomorrow.' With that, he leaves, locking me in the folly.

I scoured this hallowed place for clues once before, but now that I have unlimited opportunity, it feels wrong. I'm not usually stopped by moral principles, but I ascend the stair nervously.

The facilities at The Creepers were basic and unreliable. In comparison, the folly is a palace. I have arrived with nothing but a book, so hope that Robin won't mind if I use her belongings. Last time I was here I was disparaging. Strange how different I feel today. Wherever she has gone, she has left her overnight stuff: toothbrush, nightclothes. Sheets rumpled on the bunk. A hair on the pillow. I am the unexpected burglar, the interloper. It hasn't stopped me before. I wash, clean my teeth and look for somewhere safe to put Reginald's book.

Drawing the blind across, I cast my eyes upwards and spot a small loft hatch. Climb on a stool and nudge it open. There is a storage area above my head, which seems to be empty, so I push the book, still wrapped, into the space, replace the hatch and sit on the bunk.

Gid implied that Robin is ill. Is she in a hospital somewhere, or convalescing? It must be bad or they would have looked after her here. I lie under the blankets in my runners' clothes, close my eyes and imagine that I am Robin. Count, breathe, count, relax. I have a precious piece of coastline and have found solitude, with the people who I care for, and who idolise me, just up a path, all busy with their projects. Then I remember the guards and barriers up at the road, and the images of this very folly appearing all over social media. I slide into Robin's skin, and I know why Robin has gone. Her dream has spiralled out of control.

I need to relocate the focal point for her, away from Caernef. I must create a fresh public image. It needs to be in a city, or an earth. Somewhere symbolic for the final nine days of the campaign. But I cannot be the figurehead. I would simply be re-arrested and everything would fall apart.

. . . .

It is morning. Nathan arrives at the folly before Gid, and knocks loudly before turning his key in the lock. He enters, calling jovially, 'Miranda?'

I'm up and dressed, still thinking, and watch him light the stove. He has brought hot Caernef bread, which we eat while politely talking about the weather.

Once the tea is brewed, he asks me again about the glitch, but I counter by encouraging him to tell me about his wizardry with the okes, the runners and the nationwide delivery system. He proudly describes how it ballooned from his initial idea, and how the key was businesses jumping on board, and the proliferation of out-of-the-box commercial thinking.

'You see Miranda, take The Creepers, where you were billeted, we rent the upper floor from the absentee owner for a peppercorn. It's actually all above board, contracted, signed and sealed. There's even insurance. Assistance from the law firms was vital.'

'Hold on Nathan, so you are telling me that a derelict cottage which I thought was illegally requisitioned by runners, is actually part of your property empire?'

'Not empire. We just rent. For a peppercorn. The owners like the security.'

'But why?'

'The runners are our real-life computer game. The danger level is fabricated to provide an incentive for the young recruits. Neat.'

'So the whole runner system is a sham.'

'Not at all. It is a pragmatic solution to the nation's unemployment programme and provides an indispensable service for people who choose to relocate to the earths, as well as the #isolators in the villages, towns and cities, across the land.'

Surprised yet impressed, I ask, 'Why are you telling me this?'

'Because you asked, and because we have been led to believe that the solution lies in your hands. You need to know the truth Miranda.'

'And you trust me with this information? I could take it to the very tabloid journos who lurk outside your new barriers and watchtowers. I could screw the lot of you.'

'You could, but you won't, will you? I know that you won't do that.'

'How? Why?'

'Because you want to change the world too. You *understand*. You might tell us that you are a callous schemer, but it's a front. I can see what you really believe. You're quite like Robin these days.'

The audacious assertion that I am like Robin needles me, and I frown, but decide to give him the floor, as his brutal honesty seems genuine. 'Tell me more.'

'You and Robin are both angry, brave, creative, and proud loners. You both take control. Unlike her, you had a tough start in life, like many of us rebels, so you're more authentic. You should listen to Robin talk about this, when she's back.'

'Where is she?'

'Look, I don't know just now, but she's not in a good place in her head.'

'Her nirvana has become corrupt.'

'Something like that. And her best friends have been the cause of it. That's tough.'

Nathan turns to look me straight in the eyes, 'You do know, Miranda, that it was my solution to open the digital box which originally enabled the government to stop the glitch? I suggested it to Robin before she went to London. I've never told anyone else.'

'No?' I respond, puzzled by this revelation. What exactly was the solution then?'

'It was a simple code, converting Poppy's name into digits. Took me ages to work it out, thinking myself into the mind of the man who set it all up, Todd Humboldt.'

'There was a substantial reward for solving the puzzle?' I quiz him further.

'Robin refused it. You know how she is about money. But these days I often think about all that I could do with it …' Nathan's voice tails off. I think he is regretting confiding in me. Sounds like he is not quite as confident about relinquishing the reward as he was in his younger days.

'You see,' he adds wistfully, 'you see Miranda, we solved the cyber-terrorist's hack. The glitch should have been dead in the water, but as soon as those government people were into Todd's box, it came back. The glitch started up once more. It is as if they took over control, and started using it themselves … and from what you told us yesterday, that is exactly what happened. We all thought that Robin had stopped the glitch. I secretly knew that she couldn't have done it without me. But all that we did was give the government control.'

After an awkward silence, I ask, 'So, what's the plan now then Nathan?'

'There is no plan without Robin. It is as if the stream has run dry. We are confused, bereft, but the system which we have created carries on under a new power: people power. It is bizarre. The runners were my idea, but now they are their own idea. It's like a piece of cyber-tech which has flipped into being its own master. Help us, Miranda, please help us.'

'I … I don't yet know how. What do *you* think needs to happen, Nathan?'

'The election is a distraction. #Spoiler is already in the bag. Have a look at the data. All being well, we should shift the government without breaking the law. It was carefully planned. The question is, what next?'

'And …?'

'That's what you are here for. Anyway, tell me about this supposed murder. Gid says you didn't do it, so what's going on? You'll have to come clean with us.'

'I'm so weary of that. I was in the wrong place at the wrong time. I fired a warning shot. I didn't do it. I'm absolutely sure of that.'

We both leap up. As I say the word "shot", there is a loud banging on the door. It's Gid, who bursts in. 'Morning guys! Nathan, you've beaten me to it. Any coffee?'

Gid perches awkwardly on a stool while Nathan makes him coffee. They have done this before, with Robin, squeezed into this little room, with the stove roaring. I watch the ease with which they talk. I am the cuckoo in the nest and decide to assert myself, 'What's the plan then?'

Gid takes off his hat, grasps the steaming mug, and explains. They need me to lead their morning meeting. They need a plan, but I cannot stay here long. For one thing, the press is invading every patch between the branches with zoom lenses and instant posts, not to mention the motor launches in the estuary. Never have I had to think so deeply and quickly. Robin's alternative vision could come tumbling down at any moment if we do not act decisively.

Something beeps in Nathan's pocket, they swig the drinks and leap up, telling me to come up to the cottage in half an hour. Door bangs. Alone. Again.

I stand at the window, staring towards the estuary. The tide must be on its way out, as the rocks are wet. Wading in the rock pools is a solitary bird with a long beak, its shrill call piercing the air. Deceptive serenity. It is startled, flaps into the air, disturbed by activity on the ring of boats out on the water. A multitude of lenses turn towards the cliffs of Caernef. More characters on the board-game of life, like the runners.

. . . .

I take a leaf from Robin's book and open the meeting by getting them to talk. I listen.

It's clear that the technology out here at Caernef isn't a patch on the kit at The Creepers. They are actually more out of touch than I realised. Nathan's right. This thing has taken off under its own steam. The Caernef gang is left behind, anachronistic and baffled by the success of Robin's futuristic ideas.

They are putting out old shots of Robin to encourage

115

the runners, but there's unrest. Astute runners like Matt can sense that something isn't right. We cannot afford any internal turbulence for the next nine days. The #isolators are rebels, feisty and challenging. Need to keep them onside. We must wait for #Spoiler to come to fruition. Once the election is over, we will be able to focus properly on how we want to play Nathan's game of life. As I listen to their debate, catching the look in their eyes, our immediate move becomes clear to me.

'Close Caernef. Do it straight away.' I tell the assembled company.

Stunned silence.

'Christ Miranda, we didn't invite you here to tell us that,' Gid protests.

'Let me explain. Caernef is in danger of becoming the very antithesis of Robin's vision. Instead of a peaceful off-grid haven, far from the pressures of society and politics, this beautiful place is besieged.'

'Yes!' Glyn gets it.

'Reclaim Caernef. Send the journalists somewhere else. They must be fed up with the cold and damp winter weather out here. Get Caernef back to what it was, and carry on as you were before. Do it for Robin.'

'Totally reboot,' Nathan is onside.

'Sounds good, but how Miranda? It's easy to say.' Gid is giving me a chance.

'It's December, you can't have many more school visits until the spring?' Glyn confirms this. In fact, the group in at the moment leaves today and the camp can be mothballed until February half-term. Just shut everything down.'

Glyn takes up the story, 'I've been wanting to give Thomas and Maria some time once the baby is born. I will organise parental leave.'

Gid is sceptical, 'We would have scaled down anyway. We're not going to get Robin back that easily. The paparazzi simply won't go away. Tell us something new Miranda.'

I pause for effect, and turn my eyes on Gid as I

announce, 'The runners want Robin. The #isolators want Robin. She has been gifted the celebrity status which she so despises. We will give them Robin, for nine days, the Robin of old, the angry Robin, the visionary Robin, and if she cooperates for nine days, we will give her Caernef back, and she can be rewarded with the social oblivion she seeks.'

'Bribe her,' Gid contributes.

'You could call it that.'

'Is she up to it?' Maria asks Eva directly.

Eva has sat silently throughout the meeting, nodding, listening, smiling encouragingly. She chooses this moment to speak. 'I can persuade her. Disband the meeting, give me an hour, and I will come back to you with her response.'

So, Robin is nearby. Just as I guessed. 'Eva, I want to see her.'

'No Miranda. That wouldn't work at all. Trust me. Take a break.' Eva rises, putting her colourful coat on, to a cacophony of encouragement from her friends. Tempted as I am to track her, to discover exactly where I can find my nemesis, I know that I must wait. Patience is not my forte.

I call Nathan over while the others take a break, and we discuss options. He has several embryonic earths in his pipeline, not yet populated, but legally constituted. He can call on some sophisticated equipment as long as he gives the companies the publicity, and at this time of year, they are keen for the business. If Robin is on board, Nathan can set up the spectacle. A week of publicity. A final push across the line. But I need to create a distraction to lure the press away from this remote Welsh headland. I know what I must do. Just need Robin to play ball.

The time drags. Everyone is excruciatingly friendly. I am offered tea, cake, anecdotes and mementos. Poppy sits adoringly beside me, showing me her collection of feathers with the irritating chatter of a six-year-old. All the while, my head is buzzing. Tactics.

Eva is true to her word, and returns within the hour. She squeezes into the sweaty room, and takes her place in the centre of the group. I read her face, which is relaxed, expectant. She has succeeded, I know it.

'Friends, I won't beat about the bush. Robin is on board. She has asked for various requirements, which I can handle, including a promise, in writing, that following the election, Caernef will be protected from … from the madness of being in the spotlight. She wants a protection clause. Something about money which I have to confess I didn't fully understand. Anyway, Robin doesn't want any. She just wants the peace and quiet.'

I check with Nathan that he knows what to do. I check with Eva that she can handle Robin. I leave them to their excited planning, and I motion to Gid to come into the kitchen with me. I can't risk us going outside. Too many cameras with zoom lenses.

Gid looks anxious. 'It's all very well,' he starts, 'But you've seen the invasion of press. They're not going to go away just like that, to report on Robin making speeches in a field near London.'

'I know. That's what I wanted to talk to you about.'

'Oh?'

'You and I are going to stage the arrest of the century. We'll lure the press away from Caernef.'

'What? Explain woman!'

'I'm wanted by the law. It was all over the papers from what I heard. Let's give them an exciting escape story. They will soon jump ship.'

'Go on.'

'I've been thinking, we need a dramatic location within an hour from here. Do you know the Barmouth bridge?'

'Yes …'

'Can you get me there? On the bike? Once I'm in place, on the bridge, we will need someone else – a disinterested party – to tip off the law. They can surround me from both ends of the bridge. In fact, if you drop me on to the estuary at the southern end of the bridge, towards the ferry, I'll stage a run over the sand. Just imagine the helicopter shots there.

Remember *The Prisoner*? You'll soon see the press launches disappear from the waters at Caernef as they pile into helicopters. What haven't I thought of?'

'One very basic thing. You'll be back inside. You're willing to take that hit? For *Robin*?'

'Yes.'

'And another thing. You must get out of the runners' suit. Would create terrible publicity if you were caught in that.'

'Yes.'

'Miranda, are you sure about this?'

'Yes Gid, I'm sure. Can you get me clothes? There's no time to lose.'

BARMOUTH BRIDGE

Robin's jeans are too tight and her jumper smells of woodsmoke, but I won't be wearing them for long. I'm watching Gid's bike disappear into the distance. On my own with this now. Said no goodbyes at Caernef.

Tide on its way in. Planned precisely. Avoiding any possible cameras. Must head, unseen, for the rocks, and take cover for the count down. Then a mate of Gid's in Oxford, who he insists we can trust, will tip off a local contact, who will phone the police. I must simply wait. When I see activity, I will lure them. And then it's up to me when to swim, and to run, exposed over the sand and under the bridge. I'm ace at climbing and am looking forward to getting up on to the bridge itself. Have studied the wooden support structure on my phone. Then set up the shot. Stage a fight for the cameras, and submit. Not thinking beyond that.

Somewhere, Reginald will watch the footage, which will no doubt play over and over.

Create your own future.

Making my way, as if I am a hiker, along the path and on to the rocks. Midday sun. Bedraggled winter tourists. Turn to look at the old bridge, majestic. Nearly half a mile of timbers and iron spanning the Afon Mawddach. Must take care not to get sucked down into the estuary mud as that would spoil the story. Treacherous out here. Should beat the currents. Thought of that too.

Reach the rocks and sit, enjoying the view out to sea. No phone. No oke. Nothing. Just me and nature. Watch out

Miranda, or you will become *her*. Become Robin. No, because she is good, just, kind, selfless. Miss squeaky clean. I am the rough tough city kid who ends up in trouble and one day will overstep the mark. Maybe I have used my nine lives. Perhaps this latest scrape is it. A lifetime inside because *they* think I did it. Or sink, a failure, to the bottom of the Afon Mawddach.

Meanwhile the nation is unwittingly poised on the brink of change. The surge of silver. Eco. Futurist. A new way of living. And I dodge in and out of it, playing my part. This time creating the most audacious of diversion tactics. Luring the Caernef oglers away so that Robin can eventually return.

As planned, I slip behind the rocks out of sight and wait for the tide. Smell of fish. Slap of water on rock. Slimy under me, and spikey barnacles. I'm confident that I gave Robin's crowd what they wanted, booting them on to the next step. Nice people. Beautiful people with ideals. Loyal, unlike me. Sorely tempted to stay.

I peer between rocks. Remember the barge on the Thames. Caractacus coming to my rescue. They will punish me for that escape. On the wrong side of the law on that occasion. If they force me to answer their questions now, they could unravel the tissue of lies which has been my life. Other people's secrets, stored up. Deceptions and audacious risks. Split loyalties and last-minute switching of sides. Fickle bravado. So many times, cold, wet, clock-watching. Waiting.

But this is different. Not acting in cold blood. Not being paid to spy. Not even pretending to support the ideals of a random would-be hero. I'm doing this for her. For Robin.

"Authentic", Nathan called me. An authentic criminal: low-life. Despite all my efforts to put that behind me, here I am awaiting arrest for dirty and despicable acts, guilty of a life-changing, potentially devastating and stupid error.

The rocks are now encircled by ice-cold seawater. Urgent waves, surrounded by the invisible power of moon and tides. Soon. Must be soon. Stay alert.

The unmistakable sound of distant rotor blades. I'm ready. The question is whether someone has seen me and alerted the coastguard, or whether it is the police, and, of course, the press. This time I *need* to be on camera.

. . . .

Perfect timing. Police helicopter circling. Crouch out of sight. Wait. Wait for that second set of rotor blades. Need cameras on me before I reveal myself. Good for Gid, his contact did the trick. Now it's all over to me.

Must be patient. Surely the journalists will not want to miss an aerial adventure over this stunning Welsh scenery. Wait. Water surrounding the rocks. Crouch behind the outcrop. Wait.

Not one, not two but three helicopters suddenly circling. Gnats around rotten fruit. It's time. Lose the jumper, revealing the long-sleeved red top which will show me to the eyes of the world. This time, be visible.

I climb on to the top of the rocks and reveal myself. Don't wave. I scan the rising sea. Act as if panicking. Think of the Thames. More serious water today. Plunge in. Assaulted by the sub-zero wash. On automatic now. Swim, strong strokes. Only a hundred yards, but deep. We checked. The gnats above, desperate to zoom. Currents strong but I'm close enough and push on. Ungainly and numb, as soon as my toes scrape the mud, I scramble up, pulling feet out of sinking-sand. Triathlon training pays off. Wet clothes flapping, slowing, I run, totally exposed. Imagine the shot from above. A tiny figure striding across the sands into the hands of the law, waiting on the bridge. Starting to shake with cold. Keep moving.

Next my favourite bit. Blue lights and sirens each end of the bridge, on cue. I heave my heavy body on to the wooden supports. Colder and wetter than I imagined. Throw off the red top, a scarlet stain on the sand below as I leap up and gain a foothold. Willing my arms to work, grab, hang. Up on to the ancient slats.

Deserted sleepers: they must have closed the bridge.

Perfect. I feign panic, looking this way and that, cross the railway track, scale the low fence, and scramble on to the wooden walkway.

This is it, Miranda. Spectacular scenery spreads to left and right. Low winter sun and ice-blue water. Perfect sky. Swarming helicopters, screeching sirens. I am queen of the bridge, the hero in my own movie, hitting the front pages. Now *I* am the story, not Caernef. That is old news.

The moment is over too soon. They are upon me. I am ready for the now familiar words, 'We are arresting you for the murder of ...' But those accursed words don't come. Instead, they are arresting me under the Terrorism Act, 2022. It's a convenient catch-all. Means they can dump me in a cell until after the election. I know their game.

....

Warding off hypothermia and failing, I am desperately trying not to lose consciousness. Lying on the rough wooden bridge, surrounded by faces, lungs burning. Handcuffed, they lift me on to a stretcher and I am borne away along the old structure towards the flashing blue lights, through the baying crowds and into a waiting ambulance, where they warm me up and check me over. I feel exhilarated, a touch anarchic. A female police officer sits warily on one side, with a paramedic on the other, while we travel fast. In silence.

Job done. For Robin. Now I can sleep.

....

Hours pass and the ambulance arrives somewhere. Initially they don't know what to do with me. Brief confusion and babbling voices. Arguing over where to take their precious captive. Maximum security.

They sit me up, roughly, and open the rear door. Hordes of journalists surround us, birds of prey ready to peck. Paramedics transfer me from ambulance to security van. I don't hide my face. Shoved on a bench in the back of the wagon, still handcuffed to the policewoman. Again, that foul stink of bodily fluids and disinfectant. Voices on her radio. She's looking at a phone. Turns to me and shows me the screen. News headline, "The Spy Who Came in from the Sea," with a short clip, an aerial shot. A tiny red figure on a vast stretch of sand.

'Blimey.'

'You wanted fame?' she sneers.

'Where are we going?'

'You don't need to know. Back inside where you belong.' A cruel voice.

Where I belong? Where do I belong? For years I belonged in cheap hotels and rented bedsits, on the dark streets, in the dark web, armed and invincible. But lately, I'm drawn to Caernef. Even the smell of damp leaves, woodsmoke and rain lures me now. I realise that it reminds me of a glimpsed previous life where I was briefly safe, fed and loved. Something I've aggressively denied.

Jolt to a halt. Dragged from the van and through anonymous back doors labelled "High Security". Antiseptic corridor. Into a cell. She detaches herself from me. Click of locks. This cell is more comfortable than before. I sit on the low bed, which is covered in a crisp sheet and regulation blanket. There's even a pillow, with a clean pillow case. The toilet is in a separate cubicle. An empty desk. Civilised incarceration. Hope I stay here a while.

After some time, two uniformed guards unlock and enter. Body search and registration process is completed, but I have no belongings to hand over this time, and they leave me to squeeze back into Robin's tight sea-soaked jeans. It's not cold, but I ask them for a jumper. Want to be treated like a human being.

It takes them a long time, but one of them returns with a clean new-looking black sweat top for me, as well as food and water. He leaves. Robin's voice, nagging me to eat, so I do, and lie on the bed. Drifting. Running the events of the last day through my mind. Proud. Curious. Oddly calm.

Late evening, I guess, and I have a visitor. In officer's clothing, she enters briskly, announcing, 'Good evening

Meredith Brenton, or Miranda, I'm your welfare visitor.'

'Hi.' Aware we will be on camera.

'I will be allowed to drop in periodically. My function is to ensure your wellbeing. You are probably aware that there are delays in the courts. You're likely to be held here up to the wire. Fourteen days. So better get comfy.'

'Okay. Suits me.'

'Food will be provided. You answered the catering questions at registration?'

'Yes.'

'I can get you a kettle, mug and tea bags if you sign a form agreeing not to abuse the privilege, but milk is tricky.'

'Thank you. Yes please.'

I ask her name: she is called Crystal. She rattles on about routines and regulations, and then she turns to look me in the eye, 'I can obtain books for you to read. Classics.' She places her hand casually across her mouth, with her back to the surveillance eye, and whispers, 'Anna Karenina, for example.' Returning to official mode, she continues, 'And I can get you a tv. These are all privileges which will be withdrawn if you overstep the mark. Like the showers.'

'I need a shower.'

'You'll have to fill out a form. They'll probably let you have one tomorrow.'

'Thanks Crystal and yes please to the tv and books.' She winks and sails out through the multi-locked door of Hotel California. Either Anna Karenina has blown, and Crystal was being ironic, or she knows, and is treading a deceitful path like me. Everything about her manner was open. No jibes, no glares or looking down her nose at me. Maybe that's just her job, maybe she's a better actor than me. Maybe she's really on my side. Not sure.

An old-style tv arrives in the arms of a silent guy in overalls. He fiddles with the connexions and it flashes into life, showing adverts. Once he is gone, I familiarise myself with it, and tune into a news channel. I don't have long to wait to see my story. Fantastic shots of the estuary, zooming in on the tiny character standing on the rock, following me as I dive into the foaming sea, the voiceover explaining that the police have foiled a plot involving serious high-level espionage. I swim. They zoom in further. I can taste the salt of the water as they show my gasping mouth. At the moment when I emerge from the waves, athletic and dripping, they cut away to the bridge, showing the brooding presence of police, the lights and heroes of the law waiting to pounce. Back to me, a long-shot as I glance this way and that, caught on the bridge, and the moment when I was wrestled to the ground, with the caption, "Gotcha!".

Shots of my bedraggled body being roughly dragged from the ambulance to the police van. Today, I am one of the most wanted women in the country, finally trapped and detained ready to be brought to trial for espionage. For espionage? What of Jennifer Hayward?

. . . .

Robin updates me. She appears on the screen, standing with her characteristic air of gentle belligerence, in front of a spectacular view over distant rooves, streets, old chimneys and church towers. A vast carpet of urban living. Clever Nathan: I'm not sure *where* she is, but it's an inspired choice.

Hell, she's being asked about *me*. Interviewer: 'So we have been told, by an undisclosed source, that you know Meredith Brenton, the undercover agent who has been captured so dramatically by the government's anti-terrorist unit. Do you know that woman?'

'I know her. I travelled with her during the second glitch a couple of years ago.'

'Do you believe Meredith Brenton, the sophisticated cyber-terrorist, said to be a spy in the pay of China, to be the mastermind behind the glitch?'

Bloody Hell.

'I have no evidence of that, but I am not here to talk about the glitch, nor Meredith. I am here to talk about the General Election only nine days away, about the gathering momentum for change in this proud nation.'

Proud nation my foot. She looks the part, her hair blowing in the breeze, her eyes steely blue, boots and jeans. Like the ones I am wearing. *Her* jeans. She's visibly a misfit, bold enough to speak out, and adored by all the closet and aspirant mavericks out there. She's just an odd but ordinary person with a conscience and the courage to challenge the status quo. It's no wonder she's gathered millions of followers in such a short time. She has credibility and honesty, unlike me.

The interviewer is uncomfortable in Robin's determined gaze. More talk. Tension. Rising tones. Robin having the final word, 'The people of this country want to be governed with integrity. We are weary of deception and inept leadership. First Brexit, then the pandemic, and then the glitch. It is a woeful track record and I make no apologies for saying it *as it is*.' The interviewer hastily hands back to the studio.

Switch channels, and there I am again, the escaped spy being hauled in by the triumphant security services. And then Robin, at Rivington Pike wherever that is, telling the nation that we owe it to the generations of the future to protect our environment, to value truth and to empower small voices, offering fulfilling futures to our young people. As she says the word "empower", she punches the air. It's not for show, but because she is wrapped up in her narrative. The charismatic un-celebrity.

Switch channels. A different interviewer tries feebly to corner her, demanding that she comes clean about her opposition to the democratic process. Robin is prepared for this, and commits resolutely, 'Of course I believe in the democratic process. I support free universal suffrage, and always have done. We've made no secret of the Spoiler hashtag. The courts have agreed with us that it is a legal option for voters who are faced with an array of candidates with whom they do not agree.'

She's good. It irks me to admit it, but the strength of her voice, the slight tremble of emotion, because it really means the world to her, and her empathetic assertiveness, it's very moving, as is her total disdain for the interviewer. It will go down well. If I had a phone, I know that I would be seeing mass likes and retweets. She continues, 'This is a quiet revolution. This is a silent uprising. There are many of us who do not want life to continue in the same old way. We want change, and we want it now.'

I hit the mute and reflect. All being well, I will be able to keep up to speed through news reports. I'll simply have to read between the lines. The press seems to have stopped broadcasting off Caernef, so my act of self-sacrifice may have been vindicated.

Robin is somewhere called Rivington Pike, and she is on form. Eva and the others must have dosed her up, or talked her round from whatever 'illness' she was suffering from. I know that #Spoiler is on track, so that is a waiting game. As for my various crimes, I am baffled. Never had much to do with China, and as for being responsible for the glitch, the opposite is true. My time has been spent trying to *stop* the glitch.

There must be some significance in this mention of China. And why has Jennifer Hayward's name disappeared into oblivion all of a sudden?

Eyes peering through the grill in the door.

I ask the eyes, 'I want to see the duty solicitor. Please.'

'No solicitors are available at present. They have been recalled by the government.'

'What?'

'Blame that Robin and her #isolators.'

'Why?'

'I'm not here to talk. I will put your request for a solicitor to the boss, but don't expect one soon.'

Transfixed by the shots of me at the Barmouth Bridge, and the endlessly replayed videotape of Robin, I am gripped by the commentary and the wild theories about my crimes. Focused on the screen for the remainder of the evening. At ten o'clock the power is switched to night-time mode, the sockets are disabled, and the screen goes blank, so I try to sleep. However, the combination of a hideously uncomfortable sleeping platform and my alert brain, results in only snatched bursts of unsatisfactory rest.

Piecing it all together in the darkness. They must *want* me to be associated with China. Presenting me as subversive. Anti-British. But ... my mind returns to Robin's shipments of painkillers and stimulants, Caffeine and even codeine doled out to runners to keep them alert, and to steer them off alcohol. There's something bizarre about eco-warriors using prescription drugs, and Chinese ones at that.

Heartily relieved to see the faint signs of the sun rising, and at eight o'clock the lights blast out again.

Forcing down prison breakfast, I settle in front of my window on to the unravelling election. Nothing new. I am still a headline and clips of Robin are playing on all news channels. "This is not about party politics. I do not speak for the right, the left, or the centre. I do not speak for libertarians or for socialists, I speak outside those conventions. I speak as a human being, a human being who is frustrated by the hypocrisy, and who desperately wants society to wake up to its responsibilities."

It is the current footage of the streets which interests me. This morning in the grey December rain, gathering crowds across the land, chanting "We want change," and waving ramshackle silver-grey placards bearing the ubiquitous #Spoiler. A pastiche of shots, starting with the sea of tents on Parliament Square, more in front of Holyrood, semi-permanent gatherings on the steps of the Welsh parliament, and protestors lining the grand approach to the Northern Ireland assembly. All supporting the silver revolution. Runners flit through the background, shimmering flashes against the damp grey.

A member of the cabinet blusters on the back foot, 'We will not let these protestors erode the democracy of our great country.' He doesn't know how carefully the #Spoiler has been coordinated. It's been a quiet but thorough campaign, largely under the radar. Right now, hundreds of thousands of completely legitimate spoiled ballots will be winging their way through the post. Robin's secret weapon. Only a few of us understand the extent and the likely impact of this legal subversion.

I gasp, as I see another story running in the tabloids. On front pages. Maybe an attempt to discredit me, or maybe simply smutty journalism. Apparently, a photographer screen-shot me as I emerged from the water, Barmouth Bridge blurred enigmatically in the background. It's undeniably a really sexy shot, wet clothes clinging to my lean figure, nipples through the red top, my hair wild, my face composed. But it captures a strange smile. I am clearly thoroughly enjoying my extreme sport. Not sure whether is it an image which makes me proud, or whether it is an unsettling insight into the real me, which I thought I had kept well-hidden. Reginald will secretly enjoy it wherever he is, with his … usually … arms-length, genteel and vicarious pleasure in the female form. I miss him.

Regret.

I certainly hadn't intended to become the tabloid pin-up girl of this election.

#STOPTHEGLITCH

But what has happened to Jennifer Hayward's murder investigation? So far, I can glean nothing from the news on the tv. I daydream that this is now considered a closed book, that they have discovered the true murderer, but that's not likely. I want to wipe that night out: press delete and start again.

The tv news channels drone on: globalism under attack, freedom of information, the human rights of prisoners, lost dogs and fly-tipping.

I'm not like Robin. All this solitude and time to think doesn't suit me. Feels like I'm standing still, or even worse, travelling reluctantly backwards. I'm an action man. I thrive on activity, fulfilling my brain as I make the connections, assess the people and plot the strategy. Strange to be a detached and passive observer of what I believe to be the biggest coup in recent British history. One in which I have played a passing part.

The election build-up is bizarre. "Only a week to go," emblazoned on the screen, and endless reports from keen journalists citing an outcome on a knife-edge, a possible hung parliament. Frantic rosetted party members of all hues, except silver, scurrying from doorstep to doorstep in the mistaken belief that it will make a difference. Nathan knows. Robin knows. I know. #Spoiler went viral in the precise window for postal votes. The earths, and the #isolators jumped on board. The runners coordinated. We quietly targeted the marginals, and roused the disaffected elements in the populace. This time social media will prevail. Door to door canvassing is a thing of the past. This time, the final week of campaigning is too late.

Would-be politicians jostling for power. Extravagant statements to camera. Seeking soundbites. Promising ambitious eco-targets. Promising lower taxes and a growing economy. Promising help for the vulnerable. All missing the point that hundreds of thousands of so-called vulnerable people have *already* voted. Endless semi-celebrity influencers spouting platitudes, but seemingly unaware of the forthcoming tsunami of #Spoiler postal votes. I consider whether we want them to realise, or whether it is in our interests for them to remain wrapped up in their own illusory battles until election night, when all should unravel.

I revel in the prospect of seeing their faces at the moment they realise their pumped-up bureaucratic system has failed. I sound like Robin.

Now glued to the screen: my new reality. "The Spy who Came in from the Sea" is still running, with minor updates. Someone has tweeted the tabloid image with the caption, "How to solve the glitch."

How to solve the glitch. That's familiar. The exact words I posted with the image of Reginald, half-naked, exposed and without his glasses. Despicable man. The reminder of that image makes me want to retch. Who has resurrected my slogan? I thought it had been buried by the *establishment* almost as soon as I sent it out into the ether. Can't be chance. And how does me emerging from the sea, towards handcuffs and flashing lights, solve the glitch?

Turn up the volume. "Meredith Brenton was yesterday ensnared by security services. We now hear from the National Cyber Security Centre that Brenton has been on the wanted list for some time in connection with the masterminding of the widespread series of power and internet failures over two years.' They interview an expert who is very convincing. Apparently I have been hiding out in Oxford, controlling the glitch! Footage of the upstairs room in my "home" in Summertown, just how I left it. They zoom in through the window, showing my desk. Hold on, it's not as I left it. Someone has placed items on my desk. A laptop and papers with detailed instructions on how to disrupt … they cut away before I can read it. What the hell is going on? Rather than facing murder charges, I am held on serious cyber terrorism charges, charges which have not yet been outlined to me. I need that lawyer, and quick.

The anchor in the studio switches to a story about the silver revolution. They are nervous, but don't understand what it means. And there again is Robin, not on the top of Rivington Pike this time, but on a street surrounded by runners and Christmas shoppers, all hanging off her every word. Her face animated. She is helped up on to a makeshift platform so more people can see her. She is waving at someone, beckoning them over. Crowds are gathering as if for a flash mob performance. Think I spot Gid in the shadows. Blast. They cut away just when it was getting interesting. Frustrated, I switch off my window to the world, and prepare to exercise. You never know when it might come in handy to be in top form.

Warm up gently and slide into sit ups, two, three, twenty, a hundred, panting and into squats, lunges, counting and pushing myself as far as my limbs will go. Must repeat several times a day. Get fit. Keep fit. Maybe even escape again. Stretches. Abs. Longest, highest, pumping hard. So engrossed I don't initially notice the warder at the door.

'Brenton! Hello? Brenton.' Click of keys and multiple locks being shifted. The cross face of a prison guard breaks into a smothered laugh as she sees me, no doubt red-faced, sweating and puffing. Warm down while I listen to her. Jog. Stretch.

'Shower in half an hour. Then you have been called.'

'Shower. Thank goodness. But called?'

'Called. I don't know anything more.' She leaves, clicking, closing, incarcerating me until shower-time.

I wait. Limited coverage of Robin and the silver revolution on the mainstream channels, I try Al Jazeera,

Newsnow, Russia Today. Nothing new, so grab a quick face-wash from the basin in the *en-suite*.

My eye catches a different image of Robin on the screen as I return to sit on the bed. This is excellent. Really powerful. My God, Robin, placed deliberately in some sort of barn, or stable, sitting on a bale of straw, gently holding a very tiny baby, wrapped in a white shawl. Babies usually leave me cold, but this one has something other-worldly about it. About him, I know, it is a little boy. His black eyes pointing directly at Robin's face. Can only just have been born. You couldn't make this up. There is Maria, looking tired, but radiant, holding Poppy's hand. Thomas standing behind. And Robin, speaking to camera. It will be Eva filming on her phone, I'm sure. *"What sort of a future do we want for our new generations? We are responsible for providing this little person with a sustainable, peaceful and prosperous future. He does not choose to be born into a world which is bedevilled by power games, mistrust, conflict and destruction. Now is the time for change."*

. . . .

Totally absorbed in the image, I am dragged back to the reality of my position by two female prison guards who unlock the door, snap me into handcuffs on both sides, and lead me impersonally along the corridor.

Showering while attached to others through transparent screens, is somewhat restricting, but they release my right hand, and I spend as long as I am allowed parading my nakedness to them. They do not avert their eyes. I scrub myself clean from my recent adventures, and rub the scratchy towel over my skin. They provide loose grey prison clothes. I am a number.

I am handcuffed and transferred to a heavily armoured van with obscured glass. I like to be prepared, but have no inkling of what to expect. The guards are firmly silent, refusing to answer my questions, so I sit obediently, mapping out the wisest responses to various scenarios. Most likely it is a preliminary inquisition about the murder. In which case I am entitled to representation. It might be questioning about the glitch; in which case I will have to think on my feet. Or it could be some sort of questioning about my involvement with China. They do seem blindly obsessed with that at the moment.

After at least two hours on the road, I have a seriously cricked neck from turning to look out of the obscured glass. Where the hell are we going? We stop. My minders take time out, in turn, but I am not offered a comfort break. I don't need one. Iron bladder. As we start up again, I hear snatches of voices on their radios.

"ETA 3pm."

"Maximum security expected."

"No. She is not to know."

Close eyes and feign sleep in case I can hear more. In heavier traffic now. I can tell by the stop-start progress.

"ETA 3pm."

"Handover planned to local security."

"Priority access."

"Avoid press at all costs."

The van stops. The guards stiffen. We edge forwards.

'Brenton. You are to proceed into the building with us. No funny business. Penalties for a second attempt to abscond custody would be extreme. We will be handing you over to internal security police. When it is finished, we will be taking you back. Any questions?'

I bite my tongue, remain calm, and ask nothing. Whisked out of the rear of the van, marched along a civilian corridor. Handcuffed to two women, flanked by two policemen. This is no prison. Into a lift. Looking for clues. We travel up to the seventh floor. They press close to me as we exit the lift. Four different security guards approach. H M Government on their lapels. For a moment my hands are in four sets of cuffs. I am released from my travel companions, and taken by the new gang into an empty committee room. Hate being kept in the metaphorical dark. Hate my powerlessness. But excited by the unknown, and up for a challenge. Brain on fire.

They sit me on a chair and provide a glass of water, which I drink in one go, anxious about dehydration. A guard refills the glass, but I dare not drink more as I am unsure about toilet arrangements. We wait. Notepaper embossed with gold crowns on the highly polished table. A pile of trendy glass coasters. Conference call facilities. No bars on the windows. Smell of coffee. Several clocks outside the window chime three times. Long and slow. As the final note fades, the door opens.

'Reginald!'

'Miranda.'

Reginald De Vere, suited and the same as ever before, casually approaching me, his hand outstretched. He doesn't need to speak to my guards, because they unlatch the handcuffs and stand back, joining their colleagues in the doorway.

'No time for pleasantries,' he begins in low tones, continuing, 'in a few minutes two men will join us. One is Tustian Hayward. You know him. Top civil servant. The other is a highly-regarded aide to the Prime Minister. You do not need to know his name. They have a proposal to make to you. I strongly advise you to accept it. And Miranda …'

I will never know what he would have said, as the door flies open and two men, deep in conversation, stride into the room. Reginald subtly detaches himself from our brief tryst just in time, planting himself at the opposite end of the table, studiously ignoring me.

Reginald's presence has awakened a sparkle in my eyes. I remember my many achievements in his tutelage, and I sit proud, anticipating the *offer* with great interest.

Tustian takes charge. I have worked with him before, before … I instantly think of Jennifer, his daughter who I only saw once for a brief and fatal instant, and I wonder at Tustian calmly occupying the same room as Reginald.

'Meredith, Miranda, it is good to see you again, although your choice of attire leads a lot to be desired.' His attempt at a joke breaks the ice, he asks the guards to wait outside the door, and he gets straight to the point.

'Reginald and I find ourselves facing a dilemma, and we are keen to recruit your cooperation. This conversation is off the record.'

I glance at the video-conferencing equipment. Reginald unplugs the receiver.

'You'll just have to trust us that this is absolutely off the record.'

Trust no one: my mantra.

'Miranda, you know, and we know, that since the initial cyber-terrorist attacks, called the glitch, the government has taken the initiative. The many glitches since those early days have been controlled from within Whitehall. We will not go into why here. That is not relevant to our conversation.'

From the horse's mouth. No wonder they don't want this recorded. *Not relevant to our conversation*. I will him to spill the beans.

'We need you to take full responsibility for the glitch …'

'But …'

'Hear me out. We want you to admit to controlling the glitch and we need this to occur before voting closes on 12th December. As early as possible. Tomorrow.'

Reginald's turn to speak, 'If you oblige, you have our word that no charges will be pressed for … for any of your recent acts. By nine in the morning of 13th December, you will be a free *woman*. Until then, you will be detained, with privileges. No questions asked. You will leave all communications and press releases to us.'

I look towards Tustian, seeking confirmation, which I receive. The aide nods.

'I accept.' No-brainer.

They leave. It's over far too soon.

With renewed confidence, I request a visit to the ladies' before we leave, and am escorted by the two female guards. No handcuffs. One gives me a perfunctory shove into the centre cubicle. I sit on the toilet, and after urinating with immense relief, hold my head in my hands, processing what happened. I have a part to play. I take total responsibility for the glitch. It will forever be on my shoulders, to protect a government which I do not support. Under no illusions, I can see there is no reconciliation with Robin on the horizon now, and I will have to spend the rest of my life bearing a secret. A huge secret. How will they manage my new identity?

As I flush the toilet it occurs to me that they will probably haul Robin into the conference room too, off the record. Of course, Reginald will bribe her with Caernef. I can hear his smooth-talking in my head: *call off #Spoiler and we will ensure that you can live out your days at Caernef, that the camp will be allowed to return to the rural idyll that you sought.* Bastards. They will, I know it.

Turning to face the back of the toilet door, I am ready to give myself up to my captors who are lurking outside, and nearly miss it. There, hanging from a hook, is a very small white paper bag. Like the ones kids use for loose sweets. I delicately pluck the bag from the hook and peer inside. A micro-memory card, as well as a small spherical … inside is an oke! I cannot swallow it without water. Momentarily wonder about using the toilet water. No. A swallowed oke was far from ideal anyway. I remove the contents and check the paper bag, but it is blank, wrap it in toilet paper and flush hard. The bundle bobs up and down, and mercifully disappears around the u-bend.

I have never adopted this method myself, but have heard of it being used with drugs many times. If a tampon can fit, then why not something infinitely more interesting. With the oke and the card safely concealed, I exit the cubicle. Miss Innocence herself.

As I wash my hands, revelling in the pink soap, under the eyes of the two guards, I realise that it is too late. The earths, the runners, the spoilt ballots, as Nathan said, they have taken on a life of their own. It's too late for Tustian to intervene. They cannot bribe Robin now, surely?

....

I sleep during the long haul back to the prison where I am being held, despite being packed like a sardine between the two guards. When I wake, as the van jolts to a halt, my wrists are deeply indented from the pressure of the metal and my head is throbbing. I'm hungry.

Blinking at the bright lights of the prison blasting through the darkness, I take a brief gulp of fresh air before I am hustled back into the building. My companions are tired and short-tempered. I lie low. We pass through the body scanner and of course, I trigger a weary beeping. They are irritated. Handcuffs are removed and I am strip-searched. They find nothing. Play innocent. Send me back through the scanner. More beeping. I shrug my shoulders. They ignore me.

'She was supervised directly the whole time.'

'Something's changed since we left. She was clear then.'

'Perhaps it's the machine.'

Much poking and prodding. Grumbling. Told to open mouth. Gloved hands again searching my armpits, between my toes. They decide to go no further. It's late and they should have knocked off hours ago. I am deposited in the familiar cell. Feels like home. Deliberately leave the items where they are for the present as surveillance might pick me up on the cameras. Eat. Watch the news. Nothing new. Sleep.

Distant screaming wakes me in the early hours. That seems usual here. People come and go, the hunters and the hunted, incarceration and despair. In the darkness, obscured by the blanket, with efficiency, I retrieve the oke and the memory card, stowing them surreptitiously in my shoe. Not sure how I can use them, but they seem to have been intended for me. Try to fall back to sleep but fail, so force myself to exercise, barefoot, until full power is restored, when I flop on the bed, eat the breakfast and switch the tv back on.

Nearly choke on the cold toast, as headlines blast out of

all channels, featuring yesterday's deal. *They* wasted no time. "Breaking news: spy charged with conspiracy behind the glitch." There is an official statement which talks the government up for ensuring that innocent people will no longer be victims of glitches. Some channels are headlining with, "Government promises end of glitch," and "Courageous arrest by government security services promises rosy future." They believe this to be a massive vote-winner. It would be ironic if this false story about me pushes votes beyond the range modelled in #Spoiler. The plot might fail. Robin would *never* forgive me. It's becoming very public. Perhaps I was impetuous in accepting their offer so readily. I was certainly selfish.

Yesterday's euphoria has quickly collapsed into heavy self-doubt. The loneliness of the cell taunts me, and my brain is tangled. Seeing the headlines causes waves of nauseous panic as I realise that I will be discredited in the eyes of any friends or companions who I have made over the years. It would be one thing to be blasted as a murderer. I would be removed from society for life. It would be another thing to be convicted for the dirty minor crime that I did commit, probably alongside all my other dubious acts over years of employment on the edge of the law. But to be publicly accused of masterminding the glitch, the glitch which thoroughly polluted everyday life, causing innumerable deaths, immeasurable suffering, that just isn't fair. When have I worried about fairness?

I mean, think of Matt Wolff. Think of Caractacus; they took a punt on me. They went above and beyond, welcoming me as a runner, appreciating my skills, my speed and resilience. I can hear them saying, 'Who would have thought. Thank goodness she was arrested and removed from our lives. We were lucky there.' If they see me, they will want to spit. I feel as if I have let them down when they were unstintingly brave, for me.

Robin will despise me again. Her loyal followers, the Caernef gang, will revert to their earlier mistrust, in fact they will discuss me as they sit round the roaring December fire, and they will use words like "traitor" and "defector". No chance they will ever trust me again. Gid will return to his cynical distrust of me. No more rollercoaster rides behind him.

Hayden Eckley will text Jade the runner and say, "I told you so. No one trusts her."

Who cares a fuck what other people think?

Only Reginald knows. *He knows*. Hell, I'm confused. Why is Reginald in cahoots with Tustian Hayward? I need to know. I'm left again with a useless oke and a flash card. Don't know who from. Don't actually know if they were intended for me, in a sweetie bag on the back of a toilet door in some swish government conference block.

I hear scrabbling at the door to my cell. Clicking of locks. Oh Lord, it's Crystal, all smiles.

'Morning Miranda! Oh dear; your dog died?' Without waiting for an answer, she bustles around me, unloading books and things from a satchel on to the desk. 'There. Some things to help you pass the time. Anything else?'

'Freedom.'

'Exactly.'

'Exactly?'

'You know. Now, I'm here to make the days pass more quickly. Look, I found a copy of *Anna Karenina* for you, *Les Misérables*, *Little Dorrit* and all sorts of other pastimes. There's paper, pens, and …' As my hang-dog expression lifts, she launches herself up on to the desk, whisks some black tape out of her pocket and slaps it over the surveillance lens, landing beside me with a grunt. 'There's been some very specific instructions regarding your detention, passed down from the highest level.'

I'm gobsmacked.

'Now Miranda, I've got a really busy morning today, but before I dash off, is there anything else you need?'

'Chocolate biscuits, more tea bags, some decent pyjamas, a proper sleeping bag, a bottle of Dior Poison, a

Glock, oh and a crystal ball!'

'Not much then. I'll see what I can do, but firearms are off limits of course.'

I thank her, request her roll of black tape, which she leaves as she disappears, click, clack, gone. I nearly call her back. Stupid, stupid, stupid me. The one thing which I do need is a phone. Of course, a phone.

With the tape across the camera, I relax a little. What a bizarre morning. I turn to the small heap of books, instinctively pull out *Anna Karenina*, and immediately detect something odd. It takes me five minutes to delicately peel the webbing off the spine, and to discover what lies hidden inside the back cover. After reassembling the book as best I can without equipment or glue, I lay the thin state-of-the-art mobile phone on my knee, retrieve the oke from my shoe and perform the ceremony exactly as Hayden showed me up on the moors.

BRIDGE IN THE SNOW

But there's no signal. I've spent two frustrating days fiddling and failing. After depositing a charity bag of very welcome items for me, Crystal, my guardian angel wellbeing officer, has disappeared. She says until next week. Hope I'm gone by then. At least I smell better now, and there are still enough chocolate biscuits for a banquet. I was grateful to her, but am now seriously fed up, even though the tv has been a boon. I've watched politicians spout words from streets and hustings across the land. I've watched the newsreaders smile when they report on Robin, and grimace when they mention me.

Robin must be on a pressing schedule, speaking to cameras from all corners of the British Isles. The press wants more and more of her, the strangely photogenic and eloquent angry disrupter. They have tired of the suited politicians who spout the same old platitudes. Robin brings an element of intrigue, but she plants her feet firmly on the right side of the line, taking pains to emphasize that #Spoiler is totally above-board and legal. Several top law firms are backing the campaign. She is no doubt being well-advised.

The warders are leaving me alone. Just routine delivery of meals. Nothing else at all. It's as if I don't exist. They must be following instructions from above. They haven't made me remove the tape from the camera.

In desperation, I am holding the phone high and low in a feeble attempt to get a signal. It occurs to me that there is something in the walls intended to block it. No joy. Anyway, not sure who to text. No one will want to hear from me, and I have no numbers.

Snap out of it Miranda! No use feeling sorry for yourself, there's no one to blame but you.

Well, actually, I blame that cat. I blame Reginald, Robin, Tustian, Gid, the world and his dog. How the hell has a shrewd person like me ended up trapped like this? There *must* be a way.

There may be no internet, but perhaps I can make calls. That is, if there is a contract. Enter one of my many old numbers as a test. Nothing. Come to the conclusion I've been given this thing to use on my day of escape as it's useless in this reinforced concrete hell-hole. Turn the wretched device over and over. Should have done this before. Small sliding panel reveals a card-reader. Of course. The card is still in my shoe. Feeling more hopeful than I have done for days, I insert the card and wait as the device reconfigures. Smile. I have wasted two days. Now I'm back up and running.

The mobile phone not only lights up, flashing an array of choices before me, but it is clearly picking up a signal. I cradle it in my hands, deciding on my priorities. To be honest, I don't want to talk to anyone. There's no body on my side any more. I want to *know* everything, to see the drama of the final four days of campaigning. I scour the websites, minutes turning into hours. Totally absorbed.

The politicians are beginning to suspect that #Spoiler might have more significance than imagined. A spokesperson for the Royal Mail has referred to, "An unprecedented number of postal ballots." Despite strict secrecy requirements, someone has leaked concerns that the lists of absent voters are way longer than is usual. They smell a rat, as there are fewer absent voters in some constituencies but excessive numbers in others. Some electoral officers are having to change their layout arrangements for the count, as an unexpected number of postal votes have been received. There's a degree of panic.

Robin and her followers keep emphasizing that #Spoiler means you legally submit "NONE" on your ballot paper, nothing else, to minimise additional work for returning officers, their staff and volunteers on the night.

Apparently loads of extra closed sessions for the opening of postal votes have been held, causing logistical nightmares. What no one can know, or leak right now, is how they all voted, but I guess that many of the ballots are "spoilt", largely from #isolators and earths. Confused pollsters are desperately modelling different scenarios. Meanwhile the campaign trail continues on its relentless march towards Thursday. It would be fascinating were I not holed up in a prison cell, even if it is rather more comfortable this time.

Statisticians are still predicting a hung parliament, but confidence ratings in predicted outcomes have plummeted. Parties, other than the two big hitters, are scurrying around in the hope of holding the balance of power. Robin's supporters are talking with several of them. She's mobilised celebrities, millionaires and influencers. The social conscience of our corrupt nation is speaking. #Spoiler is trending day after day.

At first, I felt jealous of her success, but my jealousy is melting away as I listen to her impassioned speeches again and again over the airwaves. It was my actions out at Caernef which booted her into this. Since Robin has been on her carefully engineered campaign trail, the press has left Caernef behind.

Despite having actually sat in The House myself, which taught me more about corruption and influence than ethics, I have always prided myself in being disinterested when it comes to party politics. Over the years, I've worked for one side, and another, not worrying about moral underpinning. Until I met Karl and was brainwashed into believing his tales of Year Zero. I have dug the dirt on those in high office without shame. But even I am being swayed by Robin's silver army. She presents localism as apolitical. There's a logic in that. She presents the future of the planet as precarious. She's right. We all know that she is right. She's compelling.

But the very time when I feel compelled to vote, I won't get to do so. Probably a postal vote on the doormat in Golders Green. Or Oxford. Or even at De Vere Stratagems. Itinerant.

There's also a growing anti-glitch fervour, prompted by my story. Politicians on the right, and the left, are uniting in their condemnation of terrorists who callously use cyber terrorism to cause widespread suffering. They're attempting to discredit Robin. Instead of being the heroic spy, my scowling image is paraded in triumph as a guilty pariah. The face of government propaganda is my face. The enemy of the state. I cynically bought my freedom. I compromised my principle to remain below the radar. No longer a first-class operator. Ultimately selfish.

Is this a battle between my self-interest and Robin's altruism, or is the battle between convention and disruption? It is certainly a battle between Robin's passion to improve the future of the planet, and an establishment using my image as a weapon.

I've ended up appearing to be on the wrong side.

. . . .

Two more days of frenetic campaigning, all viewed from my enforced isolation, through the frame of a screen, either the tv, or the phone. My entertainment is a very public battle between those who are parading me as an enemy of the state, and Robin. Am I expected to perform the ultimate self-sacrifice? Should I be relinquishing my freedom and blowing their dirty plot out of the water? Reginald has recent evidence that the glitch is now a government plot to subdue the #isolators, which is getting out of control. I wish I knew what he wants me to do. I finger the keypad on the phone, but clench my fist.

. . . .

Tuesday morning. Two days to go. The charade continues,

and my desperation for freedom to roam the streets again is building. Obsessed with the news, it is the backdrops which interest me, not the endless soundbites from Robin, but what I can see behind her shoulder, not the heavily made-up politicians, but the settings. Instead of seeing the usual tide of weary people, parents with buggies, busy workers, the heavily-muffled homeless, I am seeing fresher faces. Optimism. But I sense the presence of a threat. Robin has taken to speaking from earths, "location undisclosed". It may be staged, but the background is fascinating. Eco-houses, productive craftspeople, children playing football on rough grass. Smiles.

Nevertheless, trouble is brewing.

I can tell that Robin's bodyguards have stepped up their vigilance. She is no longer appearing in public places. The television news is reporting use of the armed forces to subdue uprisings. Social media is becoming even more toxic. For the first time today a government spokesperson talks of possible democratic suspension. They can't even subdue hysteria with a glitch this time, because I have been captured. Emergency high-level meetings. I even think I see Reginald striding purposefully as a camera scans Parliament Square.

Reginald.

I want to speak with him. My time is ticking away, and I don't know what to do, so I cling on to my peculiar routine. At night, when the power is capped, I eat and I exercise. By day, I watch through my digital window, as repression is ramped up on the streets, and those with power seek to ridicule and overcome Robin and her vast army of peaceful followers. Another day passes, precariously. The election razzmatazz starts to overtake the #isolators as the main headline, and #Spoiler is bumped down the order in the news. By Wednesday night, election fever is widespread. Tomorrow, millions of eligible voters who have not already sent their ballot in the post, will seal the country's future, exercising their democratic right. Robin's oddball followers seem strangely irrelevant. There's no reporting about them at all today.

Can't sleep. Cell dim. Tv and phone disabled until morning. An arduous wait filled with regrets. Confidence at rock bottom. Don't know if I *could* perform if I was let out of here. Lost my sense of who I am, dressed in clothes which are not my own, and inhabiting a strange twilight world of confused guilt.

Facing reality. I have no friends. There are many people who have passed through my orbit, and many who I have pretended to befriend, because it served my purpose. Don't mind being alone. But right now, my face will be despised out there. I will be associated with causing the glitch. Used to being hated, so why does it bother me?

In my line of work, you rely on anonymity. That's blown. Again. Not likely to settle down to a sedentary day job. Won't have references, so going abroad isn't an easy option. Would have to start from scratch.

Hate to admit it, but I'm drawn to Caernef by an invisible thread of hope. Last time I was there they were kind. They needed me. Treated me with respect. Listened. They were open and trusting. Even the wilderness of the headland was oddly alluring. The draw of the escapist vision perhaps. Don't be tempted Miranda. They will not welcome you now. Unless … unless I expose Tustian, Reginald and their crew of slippery bureaucrats for what they are. But no one will believe me.

I'm deep in the shit.

Will just sit it out, assuming they keep to their promise and I am free to go once the election is over. I recall Reginald's exact offer: 'You have our word. No charges will be pressed. By nine in the morning of 13th December, you will be a free *woman*.' Quaint how he emphasized "woman". I was always nagging him about his masculine collective nouns. Want to be back in those days. Wish I could wipe out the last few weeks completely and start again. I certainly wouldn't have reacted as I did when I saw Reginald with his glasses off. I would have banged on the front door until he scrambled into some clothes and let me in. I would have demanded an explanation, and had it out with him face to face, while *she* left through the side door. I would have been sitting inside with him, discussing Rupert, the flash drive, and the runner's event at Caernef, while *she* looked in through the window. Jennifer Hayward would have disturbed the cat.

....

The polls are opening. My tv lights up at eight o'clock. Just dull footage of early voters and people with torches unlocking the doors of village halls in the dark. Government prevarication, pushing this as far through the year as they could, has been rewarded with harsh December weather. People will be unwilling to turn out to vote in this bitter wind. More ground for the postal voters, for #Spoiler and Robin's anti-establishment rebels.

Dawn is late due to thick black clouds across land and sea. Rain is falling on camera lenses, barely above freezing.

The day drags as coverage of anything *political* is prohibited. Dogs tied to railings while owners vote.

Wonder where Robin is now. Probably heading back to Caernef ready to watch the tale unfold through the night, with her friends, a hearty supper, beer and an open fire. Nice for her.

I deserve my current predicament, but I am not feeling sorry for myself, because I have devised a plan.

Tomorrow morning I will walk out of here. Not a minute too soon. No way I'm waiting for their incompetent attempt to provide me with a false identity. I've organised a bag with the remnants of Crystal's booty, a few toiletries and the roll of tape. Fortunately, her bag is an anonymous brown canvas sack. I will walk out, hood up, hope I'm not spotted, and head straight for the nearest public toilet, emerging disguised: gender-change. I've lost a bit of weight, and at this time of year loose layers will cover my contours. Need scissors to cut my hair. Not allowed them in here of course.

I'll try to obtain some more suitable clothes and money for the train. I've decided to head for Oxford because I know it well, and with any luck, I can collect some stuff from my Summertown pad: money, ID, a weapon, clothes and food. By then, I'll have decided on my next steps. Seems as good a plan as any. No way I'm waiting around in this dump for an officer to drag me off somewhere. Don't trust *them* one inch.

I graze on biscuits, read and exercise until eventually the tantalising preparations for the results are made just before ten pm. Exit polls, predictions, swingometers are about to appear, when the automatic shut-off occurs, and the cell is plunged into semi-darkness. While many on the outside wait up to see the voting unfold, I am forced to sleep, because my incarceration routine prohibits any night-time use of power. Even the phone shuts down. Worse than kids in a repressive boarding school. Not for much longer though. Freedom awaits.

I'm expecting nothing to happen at nine in the morning. Then I won't be disappointed. I'm expecting Reginald's promise to fail because of bureaucracy or spite. Every sinew in my body aches to escape this place. Can't sleep. Need to sleep. Toss, turn and grind my teeth until six, when I give in and get up, wash in the dim light, and wait for full power at eight. Seems interminable. Tap my foot to imaginary music. Want to know what happened. Has Robin succeeded in legally disrupting democracy? Or, as usual, have people turned out and voted-in one of the two main parties, disappointing the other half of the country?

I close my eyes on the dot of eight, switch on the phone, the tv, and listen. "Unprecedented scenes in Westminster where it is not yet clear who will form the next government." Open my eyes and witness the bleary-eyed confusion. A #Spoiler supporter is teased out from a baying crowd by a reporter, 'It's not political, it's human,' she cries. Cameras swing round, picking up runners, younger people, older people, all wild with emotion, anticipating triumph. I don't understand what's happened and try to piece fragments of news together.

Breakfast arrives as usual, impersonally shoved in through a hatch in the door. I don't see who by. Eat while watching the news. Shots of frenetic counting. Shots of piles and piles of "ineligible" ballots. They've been told not to use the word 'Spoilt". The reporter says that hundreds of thousands of 'defaced' ballot papers have been returned in an unparalleled act of defiance by citizens who do not feel they can vote for any of the candidates. Her heavy eye make-up disguises sleep deprivation and she runs a short flattering videotape of Robin, followed by old footage of runners and a long zoom into offices where #isolators are tapping away on computers. "It is now clear that the #Spoiler sensation gained significant numbers of supporters in the final week before voting. Not only have an unprecedented number of ballot papers been returned as postal votes, but at many counts during the night, piles of spoilt ballots have exceeded expectations. Recounts are delaying definitive results, but early indications point to no overall control, with an unexpected surge in Green MPs, possibly in double figures. Green Party leaders are in surprise talks with the leaders of other minority parties with a view to a green coalition holding the balance of power." I didn't expect this.

Blimey. There will have been be partying at Caernef last night. Wish I had been there, or with Rio and the others at The Creepers. Nathan's many algorithms seem to have won through. This could be the major shift in direction sought by Robin. Fixated on the news, until they call me. I am ready.

. . . .

At two minutes to nine a stony-faced warder slides up the hatch in the door and glares into the cell. 'Your lucky day,' she shouts at me, unlocking with spite in her fingers. I scan the cell, checking, the pile of books on the desk, and a note I will leave for Crystal, thanking her. I switch off the tv, my companion, pick up Crystal's swag bag and follow the grumpy warder down the corridor. Without revealing the manic beating of my heart, I slide into a small queue of women in prison joggers with a range of privilege tops boasting, "Release", "Eat the Rich" and "Fuck China".

We are channelled through the entrance hall like a bizarre children's game, playing trains, and come to a halt at the desk. One by one the women are provided with parcels of the clothes which were confiscated when they arrived. Small trays of valuables. They sign papers and collect cash. One by one they are supervised as they change out of the prison clothes in cubicles, donning their outside identities with expectant faces. I watch from the back of the queue.

When it comes to my turn, all that is offered to me is the pair of Robin's jeans, which smell rank, and a leaflet about claiming benefits. They let me keep the prison shoes and T shirt as I have no others. I seize the initiative and trade my half-empty bottle of Dior Poison with a fellow escapee, for a plain black sweat shirt and a black woollen hat, and head into a cubicle to put Robin's jeans on.

Need to get out anonymously with this group of women. Sign papers as Meredith Brenton. Collect no cash. Stay in the huddle. Talk to someone about the weather. Aware of cameras as we emerge into the street, out through the unlocked doors. Stay as hidden as I can.

Skirt the shadows of rundown shops. Acclimatising. Enjoying the damp, cold air, vague smells of cooking and the noise of vehicles. Don't turn to look back. Ahead only. Pass a shelter for the homeless. Notice in the window of a down-at-heel hairdresser, "Free Cuts for Homeless." Bravely dive inside. Smells of chemical sprays and damp towels. It's quiet. Two teenage assistants chew gum. One glances at me, 'What d'ya want?'

'A homeless haircut please?'

Without saying anything else to me, she throws an overall round my shoulders and fetches her cutter.

'As short as you can go,' I ask.

'Bloody cold.'

'Want to look tough.'

She grins, and tells me she can do *tough*. Fortunately she asks no questions and doesn't look closely at me. Hunks of my shoulder-length hair cascade into sad piles on the grubby lino. A few more snips with the scissors and it's complete. She shows me in a mirror.

'Great. Really great. Thanks.'

That was a stroke of luck. I escape, wandering under the festive bunting stretched across the arcade, blinded by freedom, clinging on to my vigilance, hat pulled over my skinhead cut. Comfortable with my look, confident that I can blend into the scene, my next concern is getting to Oxford. I could use a winter coat too. Need a council coat rack.

Ingenuity. On high alert. Anonymous. I dart here and there, find the railway station, avoiding as many security cams as I can, wrangling with the compulsion to resort to stealing, as I have no money and no coat. Realising this isn't going to be as easy as I imagined. Before all the Caernef business, I would have slipped my fingers into pockets, or whipped a wallet from a poorly attended bag, grabbed a coat from a market stall and run, but an annoyingly, new-found conscience is preventing me. Everything is so much more difficult when you *think*. Prefer to rely on instinct. My in-bred instinct for survival, but Robin's voice. Always Robin's voice in my ear.

As a result, by dusk I find myself still wandering aimlessly, avoiding the eyes of runners, at a loss, and so cold. Don't care that there is a new green alliance about to send a representative to see the monarch. That's all people are talking about. Hungry. Losing my grip on the positivity I felt when freedom was mine again. Hate Reginald. Hate Robin. Hate the revellers and the runners. Hate myself.

Final act of desperation, approach a lorry driver in a café car park. His English is poor, and he has a kind look. He can take me to Birmingham. Climb into the passenger seat. Thank him profusely, hoping he thinks I'm male. Hoping he doesn't have ulterior motives. The cab is warm, smelling of pies and old socks. I begin to thaw out, and accept a bag of crisps he offers me. He hands me a half-finished bottle of water, which I accept gratefully. Feeling pathetic.

He heads for the M6, radio blaring, removing the need to talk. Darkness. Headlights. Unwelcome time to reflect. Too fed up to think beyond my immediate predicament. Grit my teeth and stay warm for a couple of hours until he pulls into a motorway service station, asking me where I'm heading next. I tell him Oxford. We leave the cab, and he signals for me to follow him into the diner.

All day breakfasts. He tells me to wait, and goes up to the servery, where he seems to be known. Anxious about cameras. Pull my hat right down. My driver is laughing with a group of others, gesticulating, glancing back at me.

He returns with a mate, slapping him on the back, turning to me and saying that his friend is Mo, and he's leaving now for Bicester. That'll do. I tag along with Mo, hoping his cab is warm.

. . . .

Mo drops me at Bicester Village railway station after midnight. There's a train to Oxford Parkway at ten to one. The ticket barriers are open. I lurk in shadows, eating the last of Crystal's chocolate biscuits, but they taste of cardboard and I struggle to swallow. Try to understand why I've lost all my bravado. It's Robin's fault my self-esteem has drained away. Instead of feeling a callous satisfaction in coming out on top, I find myself wondering about the impact of my actions on others. What crap. Find myself almost wishing I was back pacing the cell.

Prove that I haven't lost it completely. Hear the train approaching. Deserted platform. Dart through the disabled ticket barriers and into the train. Sit innocently willing the doors to close, my back to the glass eye in the ceiling. Only eight minutes to Oxford Parkway. Empty carriage, empty brain, empty world. Ticketless, purposeless, friendless and adrift.

Oxford Parkway is public, fenced and floodlit. Just a twenty-minute walk to my Summertown pad now. Barriers open. Walk nonchalantly through, undetected. Once on the forecourt, run. Zillah the runner. Roads I know so well. Within touching distance of the stuff that I need. Can't exist without money, coat, weapon. Need.

Jog along pavement stretching for half a mile under trees, through familiar north-Oxford affluence, passing the golf club, the sports fields, the cemetery and hoardings advertising Oxford Pride. Bus stops, traffic lights and speed cameras. Cross the A40 roundabout, always busy, even at this hour. Dive between million-pound houses, along the genteel avenues. Only one goal in my mind.

Turn the corner of the road.

. . . .

I should have known. Should have guessed. Naïve to assume nothing would have changed. Too dangerous to stay around here. Not only were security guards planted at the gate, but the gracious old building is surrounded by temporary high metal fencing, like on building sites. Floodlights and police cars.

Stupid idea to return to the exact place where they will be expecting me to turn up. Stupid. In the absence of any options, I run, automatically, pounding one foot after the other on the wintry pavements. Passing occasional night-time workers. Being passed by occasional buses. Streetlights and plummeting temperatures.

I run past bus stops, treading on cigarette ends. Past closed shops and sleeping pubs. Remembering the glitch, when I joined Robin's madcap journey and we watched the candles in the windows of the pubs where frightened crowds gathered. We have fucked this world up.

I have fucked my life up.

Keep thinking I'm being followed. Paranoid now. Shooting pains in my legs, slow to a walk, realising the inadequacy of these shoes. Porticos and cycle racks. Glow of streetlamps catching the bay windows and the chimneys.

155

Old, grand bricks and gothic architecture. Two worlds. Their world and my world.

Cross the canal. Pause. Lean on the smooth top of the old brick wall. Gaze helplessly down to the black limpid water. Canal boats in darkness - the haunts of digital nomads and those seeking no mortgage - lined up along the bank under the bare branches. Idyllic yet problematic.

Like Caernef.

Walk slowly past parked cars, on to the railway bridge. Up the line, winking red signals. Down the line, the glow of the central station. Vans. Trains in sidings.

Suddenly I remember the finale of *Anna Karenina*. When one sees the truth, what is one to do? Standing on the bridge, trying to think what I have come here for. Everything which seemed so possible before is now so difficult to consider.

Anna knew what she had to do, but even she didn't stage-manage a perfect ending. It always worried me, how she tried to fling herself under the train, but missed her chance because she was concerned about her red bag.

My bag is brown. My red bag moment was Robin's red top, dashed on to the sand as I climbed up on to Barmouth bridge. Iron rails there too.

Anna jumped because she wanted to punish the people who she loved. I remember the line, "She tried to get up," as if, having taken that final decision, she had second thoughts, but was too late.

I watch the first train of the morning creep out of the station, screeching and roaring, lights ablaze. I watch it approach the bridge, and I know what I must do. I grab the brown bag, decisively, retrieve the oke and the phone with the flash drive, heart beating in my hollow ribcage. As the engine approaches, I catch the eyes of the driver, and she sees me. She is thinking the worst, but before her immense machine clears the bridge, I drop my bag by my feet and fling them down. First the oke. Damn that Robin. Then the phone. That's for you Reginald. The train thunders through and onwards up the line, where the signal is now green, leaving them untouched between the rails.

They can stay there. A fitting end. I'm no Anna Karenina.

Drained and bereft, I stand on the bridge. Flakes of snow begin to fall gently, cruelly magical under the lights. Shiver. In no time at all, the sparkling dust becomes heavy snow, sticking to the cold, dry ground, coating the walls and railings. Madness being out in this weather. Trudge through the falling snow, my footprints being covered as I make slow progress towards the only place I can think of, the city centre.

NETTLES AND ECHINACEA

Fuck the election triumph a week ago. I'm out of it. Scavenging like a feral pigeon. Chilled to the core. Falling-in with a transient crowd of drinkers and drug-users. Refusing to participate, but paying the price. Paying the price for guilt, for my stubborn refusal to ask for help. Health declining. Lurching from one freezing night to the next. Unclear future. Bare survival.

Tonight we, that is my chosen group of street companions, are pressed under a bridge down by the water. They have lit a fire in an old corrugated metal bin, and the warmth softens the bitter taste of night. Passing round bottles of an evil colourless alcohol. Piss steaming as it hits the river. Too cold to smell. Don't eat, so don't shit.

They fear me. Hold self-defence spray under the jacket. Both stolen. Hold it until my knuckles split with pain. They fear me because I stay sober and protect my rights. Rights to a space by the fire. Don't get too close to any of them. Use their company as protection. Fair play. Defend them when mouthy thugs pass by. Face fixed in a grimace. Limbs taut, ready to spring at provocation.

Tonight the reflections of the flames dance on the water, the city skyline looming behind, with towers of *success* cradling a thin moon. Capitalist oratorio.

At dawn we disperse. Alone. Incognito. I wander slowly back towards the shops through the chill morning air. A mist rises above the water as I cross the bridge, hearing the clanking of the industrial refuse lorry. Fluorescent workers dart in and out of the backs of shops, dragging dripping wheeled bins. Pigeons peck discarded bin bags. Scruffy city streets.

Watching a woman in a dressing gown eating toast, spying through her window. Glowing rectangles reveal people getting ready for the day, their blinds open for random strangers like me to peer through. Early cafes open reluctantly. I choose one where I can get a mug of tea for 99p and sit out the first couple of hours of the day, watching keen office workers grab and go.

Empty without work. Sick without food. Lonely. Unfulfilled. Wanted. For murder. My brain isn't in the right place. I stagger out of the café and along superficially joyful pedestrianised avenues where tight-lipped shoppers celebrate their Christmas purchases. While my throat rasps, they drink mulled wine indoors, satisfied that this Christmas might be white. White. Pristine. Pure. A clean Christmas. A fresh start for a tortured country. Silver runners dart over paths cleared of snow and I shudder in a disused doorway.

Robin?

Miranda?

There was no room in the inn.

Where are you Miranda?

Why do you want to know? It's none of your business, Miss goody-two-shoes.

Where are you? Come on Miranda?

In purgatory. In a pit. In a doorway. In the shit.

Where?

In The Pike, the revellers raise their glasses and lick their lips. I stood at the bar and you slunk in. The glitch. Anna Karenina in the roof. On the bridge.

Where are you Miranda?

Little Bo-Peep has lost her sheep and doesn't know where to find them.

Miranda?

I'm on the clifftop at Caernef, looking down towards the rocks.

I'm on the top of Rivington Pike, the world below me.

Looking down.

I'm shut in the upstairs bedroom of The Creepers, looking out for Gid.

Gid?

Miranda?

We are racing the lights, riding the dragon. Late braking and dicing with death.

Where are you Miranda?

Not with you.

Where though?

Thrown in the ditch. Too fast. Too slow. Waiting. Gid, what am I waiting for?

Only you know, Miranda.

She knows. He knows. Who knows?

Miranda?

Reginald?

It's not what you think.

What? What isn't what I think? Gobbledegook.

Reginald?

. . . .

Early morning: the street is saturated from overnight rain. Sun emerging over rooftops above shops. Light from the 24-hour pizza place assaults my eyes. Debris, sodden from melting snow, decorates the gutters, and the street-sweeping machine drives towards me. Three all-night drinkers stagger past, kicking my cardboard. I cling on to the plastic sheet which served as a blanket through the night. I am a mound slumped in a doorway. Detritus.

Shrink under the municipal awning as an early-morning shape approaches, carrying a steaming paper bag. Lined face, accentuated by the street-light. Head surrounded by a halo of bright light. Expecting them to avoid me and cross the road, but they stoop, fingerless gloves, soft touch on my arm. Blink and focus. It is a woman.

She is invading my space and I grab my defence spray. We struggle. Aim to spray her in the eyes, where she is vulnerable. Cornered and at a disadvantage, I lose my grip.

She wrests the spray can from me, and places it beside me on the cardboard, saying, 'Show me your wrists.'

'What?'

'Your wrists.'

We struggle again, but waves of dizziness prevent me from defending my ground. She grips my left wrist firmly, turning it over and shining her torch on to my filthy, wasted flesh, tracing the scars softly with her fingers.

'Miranda. Have you got a phone on you?'

'No.'

'Me neither. Not to worry. We'll just have to walk.'

. . . .

Don't remember walking anywhere. Memory busted just now. All that matters is the present. The beautiful present. Too weak to walk at the moment. Seem to need to sleep. Not too weak to refuse drugs, to refuse coffee, to refuse to talk. Remembering who I am, shaking my head. Hair growing back.

Propped up on soft pillows, covered in a home-knitted blanket. In *the* bunk. In *the* lookout. In *the* folly.

Time has melted away. Through the thick glass, I watch the tides rise and fall, water birds wading and scurrying. No people. Nothing but cliffs, sea and birds. And Maria, with her little bundle strapped into the sling, baby Cai. She has taken to unloading him while she makes drinks downstairs, and I cradle him. Was unwilling at first, but it's easy once he trusts you. Mistrust, it all falls apart and he wails. Mostly I'm alone, looking forward to Maria's regular visits. She washes me, feeds me, coaxes me to sip her broth and inhale her herbs. Fresh-baked bread with leek and potato soup. They grow all the vegetables. Simple life. Like in the earths.

Not like in the earths.

Still piecing things together. Lost the ability to reason. And don't care, just enjoying drifting. She says I'm getting stronger each day. Focus on getting well again. Don't talk. To anyone. Not until I've spoken with Robin.

Robin is not here. Apparently, she sat by the bed when

161

I was ill, day after day, but once I turned a corner, she had to return to her work in London and Oxford. They say she'll be back soon. They're glowing with optimism, Maria and Thomas. No one else has come down here yet. Perhaps they're hiding me. From the law.

Seem to have picked up all kinds of infections: urine, skin and digestive. Thank goodness for Maria's patience and her plants. She is treating me as a living experiment, administering echinacea, garlic and lovage all grown herself up in the allotments. She keeps mentioning nettle tea, but apparently she didn't pick any nettles earlier in the year. Relief. I do begin to feel better. No hurry, she says.

Key twists in the lock below. A sound which still fills me with alarm. Heavy footsteps. Must be Thomas this morning. He's talking in a low voice, so has brought baby Cai. 'We will take her some nice food. Now, up the stairs. One, two, three …'

Thomas arrives in the lookout room with a waft of sea air and a tempting bowl of porridge, still steaming despite having been carried across the field to the folly. There is far too much honey on it. They are trying to feed me up. He stands playing with Cai's tiny toes, teasing him, while I eat the breakfast. I hand him the empty bowl, thanking him and taking Cai while he disappears to make me a cup of tea. I am beginning to feel well enough to do it myself. Don't trust my legs on the stairs yet.

Cai knows me now, and wriggles with pleasure as I rub his tummy. He's so much bigger than he was only a few weeks ago when I caught a glimpse of him in Robin's arms on the tv. Shudder as I think of that cell.

Thomas returns with hot tea, and manoeuvres carefully around Cai, placing my drink on the bedside table, then picking up his chortling son. 'If you want to talk …' he tries.

'I've been to hell and back,' I volunteer, adding, 'My brain doesn't seem to be in gear yet. But I will be eternally grateful to you and Maria.'

'It's no trouble. You'd do the same for us if we needed

a bit of extra care.'

Not sure the old Miranda would have done, but smile, and bravely ask, 'When is Robin coming?'

'Sorry. Haven't a clue. She's really busy in London, with the politicians at the moment. Maria says not to worry you about it. She'll be back when she can. She always comes back. Thanks to you, Caernef is relatively quiet again.'

Thanks to me. Of course, my staged escape. The red shirt, the bridge and the handcuffs. Did it for Robin.

How did she know where to find me?

I wave at Cai, and they leave me in peace. Lying back on the pillows, I stare towards the ceiling and wonder whether *Anna Karenina* is still in the attic, or whether Robin found it. Can't think of Anna without feeling the top of the wall, looking down dizzily at the railway tracks. Thought I was invincible until recently. Learning more about myself. Can't hack being totally anonymous. Can't manage failure. Need admiration to boost my performance. Need to work for Reginald.

Brisk knocking on the door. Freeze. Felt safe here. Hell, who's that. Key in door. A voice, 'Hi, Miranda?' Thud of boots. Familiar whiff of cigarette smoke. Gid stomps up the stairs. Haven't seen Gid since he dropped me at Barmouth sands, apart from glimpses on the tv. Don't feel ready for criticism. He senses fear on my face. 'Hope you don't mind me coming down? Thomas said you were looking much better this morning.'

The lie sticks in my throat and refuses to come out, so I tell him the truth. 'I don't feel ready for visitors. I can't face any challenge. Not yet. Gid, treat me kindly.'

He approaches me with an uncharacteristic tenderness, holds my face in his huge hands and laughs. 'You were fantastic on Barmouth sands.'

'I was?'

'You know you were.'

'Not sure of things at the moment.'

'Well. I'm telling you. You were amazing. And that shot

as you came out of the water. It was made for social media. Cracking. Got it up on the wall in the dormitory.'

He removes his boots, dropping pieces of stiff mud on the floorboards, hangs his jacket on the chair, and sits on the bunk by my feet, staring out of the window at the water. 'Do you mind if I smoke?'

'Yes Gid. I mind. It's a filthy habit and you should stop.'

'That's what Robin says.'

'Go on. Open the window.'

He opens the window and a blast of January air surprises us both. He lights up and the smoke blows back into the room. We both laugh. Don't remember when I last laughed. After a quick drag he throws the butt out and closes the window.

'Not one of my best ideas.' He mumbles. 'Thomas said you weren't ready to talk. I won't push you Miranda, but …'

'It's okay Gid. You are cheering me up. But I'm confused. I will need to talk, but not now. I want to see Robin first. Tell me about something interesting.'

'Nathan has designed a replacement for the oke. It was too clunky and old-tech. You should see the new version, a tiny silver bee, which you pin on to your clothes. There's a minute earpiece. He's calling it Arcadian B. It's not ready for mass distribution to runners yet, but should be within a couple of weeks.

The weariness has lifted from my body as I listen to him. I'd forgotten about okes. On the bridge. Like a dream. I threw the oke on to the rails. As soon as my spirits rise, they fall. I frown.

'What's up?'

Can't lie any more. 'I found an oke in a sweetie bag on the back of a toilet door in a government conference block.'

'Really?'

'I had to smuggle it out. You'll never guess where I hid it.'

'Knowing you Miranda, there is one place where I would have looked straight away.'

I raise my eyebrows.

'You swallowed it!' He announces triumphantly.

'Wrong. Very cold.'

'Er. Your ear.'

'Even colder.'

'Your shoe?'

'And have to waddle like a hobbledehoy?'

'Haha. Alright, you put it up your ...'

'Who *do* you think I am?'

'I'm close then …'

'Time to change the subject,' I squirm.

Gid looks at his phone and says he must dash. He's meant to be working with Glyn on the dormitory repairs. I don't want him to go, and say so. He loiters in the doorway and tells me to concentrate on getting better. I'm exhausted. Not as fit yet as I would like. Close my eyes. Gid calls back, 'Funny to see you in Robin's bunk. I once spent the night in it too.'

My eyes snap open, 'With Robin?'

He winks at me and disappears.

…………

One day becomes another, and I gain strength. Starting to crave freedom. I can get downstairs and even outside for air, although the weather is torrid. Maria, Thomas, and of course Cai, care for me well. I'm grateful. Will definitely repay their efforts one day. Not sure how.

Eva came down to see me too yesterday, bringing cake.

They are all being so kind. Still haven't discussed anything that matters with anyone. Waiting for Robin.

Strange how I have avoided any news. The very thought of social media makes me feel ill. I'm reading a lot, and beginning to think properly. Haven't looked into the attic yet. Need to know what happens next in my life. Feel embarrassed by my dependency, by the mess I sank into so quickly. Deeply frightened of being charged and sent back to prison. Enjoying my time, in the knowledge that it might not last.

I'm spending hours muffled up in woollies out on Robin's favourite bench, which is set against the outside wall of the folly, facing the estuary. I've found binoculars. Novel to be using them for bird watching rather than tracking a distant and wanted character for Reginald.

I'm interrupted by the sudden pad of small feet and Poppy arrives enthusiastically, hugging my legs and jumping up and down with pleasure.

'They let me come down to you, at last!'

'Poppy, it's lovely to see you.'

'I have been given a very important message for you. You'll never guess what!' She waits expectantly. I'm at a loss. Not used to six-year-olds.'

I guess: 'Something to do with Cai?'

'No. Try again. I'll give you three goes.'

Relieved it's only three, I try again, 'You have won a prize? Something at school?'

'No, last try.'

'Robin's coming?'

'How *did* you know, Miranda?'

'It's the thing I want most of all, so I hoped I was right.'

'Me too. But where will Robin sleep?'

'I don't know. I'm sure Mummy and Daddy will sort something out. Now, how about telling me more. Would you like a glass of milk?'

'Yes please.'

She follows me into the folly, and we settle on the kitchen bench, once I have made drinks.

'It doesn't smell of Robin any more,' She observes. Wonder what Robin's smell is like. 'It smells of Mummy's herbs. I'm going to be a herbalist when I grow up, and a teacher, and a footballer.'

'Wow.'

'What did you want to be when you were a little girl like me?'

'A spy.'

'Oooh. And what are you?'

What am I? 'I was a sort of spy, and a fighter, and a … an investigator.'

'Cool. I want to be an investigator too.'

'Poppy, what do you know about Robin's arrival?'

'Well, she's coming on the train tomorrow. Daddy is taking me to the station to meet her. Mummy is staying with Cai. Robin wants to see you. She was so worried when you were poorly. She wouldn't let any of us come down to see you.' She smiles with a knowing look, and asks, 'Miranda?'

'Yes?'

'I saw you at the runner's festival, didn't I? When I was collecting the bottles. I told Robin. You were a runner then not an investigator. I love runners. I want to be a runner when I grow up.'

She finishes her milk, thanks me politely, and says that she will be expected back at the cottage, having delivered the message. She tosses her head just like Maria, and asks me to hold out my hand and close my eyes, which I do. She runs out the door. I watch her sprint across the field up to the cottage and I uncurl my fingers, to reveal an oak apple, a real one. I wonder if she knows about Arcadian B.

....

I am under strict instructions to wait, and Robin will call for me. Hellishly nervous. Not sure why. Imagining our conversation, a hundred times over. Need to ask her about Reginald. Must remember to compliment her on #Spoiler.

....

A lone woman in wellingtons, wandering silently through the rock pools. I see her before she sees me. She can only be five-foot tall. Such a slight figure. Unassuming, in duffle coat and bright knitted hat. She stands and stares across the water, probably checking there are no photographers. She is watching the seabirds, specks on the dark grey water which reflects the layers of brooding cloud. On one hand a tranquil scene, on the other, disturbing, as a storm is clearly brewing. Don't want to interrupt her reverie.

Maybe she knew I was here all the time. She looks up to

the folly, and waves at me to come down. It's a challenge. She must know I've not been down on the rocks yet. Proud, I scramble hesitantly down on the steep and narrow path, my legs shaking, my spirit quaking. I didn't have a spirit until I came to Caernef. Gusty wind buffets my coat. Actually, her coat, which I've borrowed along with everything else. Her bed. Her most private space.

I pick my way awkwardly across the rocks, trying to read her expression as her forehead wrinkles and the ghost of a frown passes across her face. Reach her, and we embrace, silently. Long and slow. Woodsmoke in the weave of her coat. No need to speak. Nervous. The wind ruffles our clothes and she smiles.

Struggle to find the words: 'Robin, I'm very grateful.'

'It's me who should be grateful. You took the scent away from Caernef, in spectacular fashion.'

'You rescued me when I was … I was desperate. How did you find me?'

We walk, and she tells me how they tracked the oke and then had to scour the streets of Oxford. She talks of the election, #Spoiler and the appetite for change that exists, not only in the earths and with the #isolators, but everywhere. I ask whether she has seen Reginald.

'Yes, I was with him yesterday in fact.'

'You know he sent me the original *Anna Karenina*, with all his notes?'

'No! Goodness. I thought all the paperwork from De Vere had been either trashed by the anti-#isolator vigilantes or confiscated by government.'

'I put it in your attic.'

She looks confused. 'My attic? The folly attic, the one where my inheritance was hidden? I avoid looking up there now; it holds dark memories for me.'

'I thought it would be safer up there. Robin, you have it. It's better off with you and at Caernef. Who knows, one day it might fetch a welcome financial boost at auction!'

'When Reginald gains world-wide fame for stopping the

glitch you mean.'

We laugh. 'I'd like you to have it. It tracks many of my campaigns over recent years. Who knows, you could turn it into a novel one day, writing at your desk in the lookout.'

'I will take good care of it. It might answer some of the many questions I wish I had asked Reginald.'

'I still have so many questions too, but most of all I need to know, who was Jennifer Hayward?'

'Was?'

'Yes. I'm supposed to have murdered her, remember?'

'Has nobody told you?'

'Told me what?'

'About Jennifer Hayward?'

'Only that she's dead, shot in Reginald's arms, by me apparently. His naked arms. Robin, his glasses …'

'Oh Miranda. You're so out of date.'

'Really?'

'Well for one thing, Reginald took his glasses off to get a better recording. They are bugged. I'm surprised you didn't know. He needed to hear Jennifer say it. She knows you see.'

'Say what exactly?'

'Jennifer Hayward is the only person who knows precisely how the government was plunging us into a digital darkness and passing it off as an act of cyber-terrorism coming from the #isolators.'

'But Tustian?'

'Oh that's simply a coincidence. She is not related to him.'

I got it all wrong. 'And was Reginald … he was virtually naked. I saw him.'

'Gross. I know. The things he will do to obtain intelligence. I didn't think that was his style.'

'I'm meant to have shot her.'

'That's an old story Miranda. They know who shot her, it wasn't you, and she pulled through after all. Jennifer is a schemer and a survivor. Worse than you.'

169

'Not me! Not me. She's alive. I'm off the hook? I'm not going to do any scheming ever again.'

'That's a pity, because you are *so* good at it.'

'No. No, I'm not, Robin. It's a pretence. I have lied and boasted my way through. I have cheated and wheedled. The strange thing is that I'm not sure exactly why.'

'You are a good person, Miranda.'

'Really? Am I? That's you. You are the good person. Everyone loves you. Not me. I'm the pariah.'

'Rubbish. I'm as flawed as everyone else. Anyway, if you are such a bad person, why did you give yourself up to the law to protect me and Caernef. That was a selfless act if ever there was one.'

'Like Nathan giving up the reward for stopping the glitch because of his loyalty to you and your principles?'

'Water under the bridge. Hold on, how on earth do you know about that? In fact, Nathan's hunch wasn't right, but I didn't think he needed to know that.

Maybe Robin's close-knit band isn't as close as I believed. We sit on a mound of wet rocks, and she tells me about the election, about Nathan's genius and the tide of change flooding the land. I just want to know who shot Jennifer Hayward if it wasn't me.

She says, 'I didn't want any of the exposure. Celebrity culture appals me.'

'We are all vulnerable. It's not a kind world out there. So who shot ...'

'Reginald wants to see you. He will explain. He has a proposal to make to you. You're still on his payroll you know. Do you feel well enough to travel? He won't come all the way out here, although sometimes I wonder whether a few days in nature would help his stress levels.'

'He's stressed?'

'He's been through a lot lately.'

Before I can ask more questions, she strides off towards the folly, calling for me to follow. I arrive at the seat after her, my legs still frustratingly weak.

#isolate

'I love being back here, despite all that has happened,' she explains, adding as an afterthought, 'When things were tough, those wretched journalists kept dive-bombing me and we were fighting off broadsides from the anti-#isolate brigade, I often imagined I was you. I asked myself, *what would Miranda do now?* It gave me strength, and an edge which doesn't come naturally to me. It's hard to believe that you are here now too. I have always secretly admired you for your courage, and your ruthlessness. I wish I could be as tough and as clever as you Miranda.'

EBONY RUNNERS

Standing in Hyde Park with Gid, looking up at the windows of De Vere Stratagems. He is enjoying being my bodyguard, and I certainly appreciated his company on the train. Robin insisted I wasn't to travel back to London alone, and Gid has been instructed to leave me here. He is heading for a secret rendezvous to meet the eyes and ears behind the London runners.

'Gid, now we are actually here, I'm nervous.'

'Rubbish. You're not the nervous sort.'

I grip my borrowed phone, glancing for the hundredth time at the single text from Reginald, "Pick up some coffee." Normality. Can I really go back to this?

'Gid, say "Hi" to Matt Wolff for me.'

'Will do. Now, you okay from here?'

'Yes. Thanks. Have a good meeting. See you soon I hope.'

He slaps me on the back with such genial force that I have to brace my legs to stay upright, and he heads off into the distance, leaving me feeling alone and unsure.

The vestibule of De Vere Stratagems is changed. As if in a dream, I drift past the new young receptionist who guards the entrance, and notice that different pictures grace the walls up the stairway. Instead of reproductions of paintings by Constable and Rembrandt, there are a couple of framed Turner prints and a striking van Gogh. Give him another year and we might even see Picasso.

Pause on the landing. Familiar polished wood. Deep breath. Returning after a break is always difficult.

Reginald De Vere opens the door to his inner sanctum, unable to hide his pleasure at seeing me. Slightly embarrassed, he holds out his hand, and grips mine firmly, saying with irony, 'Welcome, Zillah the Runner.'

I say nothing. Sit in my usual chair at the large Victorian boardroom table and await instructions.

'Where shall I begin?' he muses, sitting opposite, staring into my eyes without flinching. 'Where shall *we* begin?'

'How about we call today Day Zero and go from there?' I suggest.

'Day Zero.' He rises, turns to his bookcase and slides out an unfamiliar tome, placing it in front of me. No title on the faded front of the book. There must have once been a dust jacket.

I open it and read the title out loud, 'Return of the Native.'

'It will be our new volume as *Anna Karenina* was rumbled. Have you read it?'

'Not yet.' He produces a paperback and hands it to me. No doubt he will have an identical copy. 'Code DV replaces AK. Diggory Venn is the hero. Would you like me to be business-like, or would you like a few minutes off the record first?'

I lean across the table, pat his hand affectionately and ask for a few minutes catching up informally first. A silence hangs between us, and he moves to the sideboard, turning on the CD player. So 90s. It is Mars, from The Planets. We used to blast this out to cover the sound of our voices, just in case we were being recorded or overheard.

Leaning on my elbows, my hands across my mouth, I decide to help him out, 'I will take you back to that night. You know I succeeded with Rupert. I came to Hampstead so I could hand you the flash drive; the one I gave you later. I stood outside your downstairs window. There was a gap in the curtains. Not like you. When I looked in, I saw you, in a state of undress Reginald, with her. With Jennifer Hayward.' He coughs with embarrassment. We don't usually discuss the personal, only the professional. 'Reginald, what the fuck were you doing?'

'Well that seems to have been obvious to you.'

Patience. 'No, no it wasn't. Your glasses off, your clothes off. I saw red.'

'That is not like *you*.'

'I fired one warning shot. A warning shot Reginald. That was all. I wanted to blast you into your senses. You looked as though you were going too far.'

Reginald rises. He goes to his desk and takes an old matchbox out of the drawer. He hands the matchbox to me and gestures for me to open it. Inside is a single bullet from my old Smith and Wesson revolver. I pick it up and look at it with curiosity.

'It was extracted from the tree outside the window.'

'When?'

'Too late. You had gone underground. They couldn't find you at first.'

'So Jennifer Hayward wasn't shot at all? You finished your love-making and she went home?'

'It wasn't like that Miranda; you remember Cairo. You remember Operation Retrieve. You know what it's like. You are the expert. I never made love to Jennifer Hayward. But thanks to your disturbance, I didn't quite finish the job which I intended.'

I smother a smile. He's not comfortable. 'What happened next Reginald? I need to know.'

'Of course. This is not easy for me Miranda. Cynthia, my wife, was disturbed by your shot, so she hurried downstairs, catching Jennifer and I in a state of partial undress. Before I could act, she had grabbed the gun she knows I keep hidden in the drawer of the dresser. She aimed at Jennifer, and fired. I didn't know she had it in her. Very unfortunate all round. She turns out to have a damn good aim.'

'Bloody hell.'

'And before you ask, yes she and I have sorted things out. It took some ingenuity I can tell you. *They* don't want anything coming out about the glitch, so we have managed to cover up for the present.'

'I'm sorry.'

'Why?'

'Because if I hadn't fired into the tree, she would never have done it, and your life would have been much easier.'

'We don't live for easy lives Miranda. You, especially, know that, which brings me to the proposal I have for you. Are you ready to move on now?'

Move on. From being Miranda, from being Meredith Brenton. Am I ready to move on?

'Yes.'

He strides to the CD player, turns the volume down, and stands with his back to the window, silhouetted against the January sunshine. I stand up too, and usher him over to the bookcase. Instinct never fails me. Don't let your mentor stand in full view of the street outside. Having discovered the truth of Jennifer Hayward from the old guy, I certainly don't want either a dramatic assassination or zoom shots appearing in the tabloids.

He stands in front of the bookcase and fiddles with his tie. 'It's Robin.'

'Robin?'

'Look Miranda, I really don't want you to think that I'm pulling you from the serious stuff. Believe me, there's plenty going on and I could use you in several parts of the world, or indeed, back here, but you are … rather well-known at present.'

'Spit it out Reginald.'

'After all that has happened, Robin needs a bodyguard. It must be a woman, and a woman with guts. It is a 24/7 role. She's increasingly vulnerable out there, and attention is only going to increase now she's on to a new campaign.'

'New campaign?'

'She will tell you if you accept.'

I cannot think of a commission which I would welcome more. 'Reginald, I've changed. No more gung-ho amoral

Meredith Brenton. What Robin is doing is transformational. I made it my business to treat her as my enemy ever since she and I crossed swords over the glitch, but things are very different now. I was wrong. You have always backed her, I know. Having been through the experiences of the last few weeks, I understand why.'

'Details are simple. I want you two steps ahead of her. I want you watching her back, and online. You need to know exactly where she is every minute of every day and night. But blend in, Miranda. *You* are not the story. There are plenty of well-heeled officials and lawless renegades who wish her harm. There's plotting and there's counter-plotting. Insiders and outsiders. I want you on top of it all. For her.

Report to Caernef next weekend There's cover until then, a chap called Paul. Instructions in the usual way. Weapon pick-up on Day One. Leave the preparation to me. You must get as deep into her campaigns as you can. Live and breathe it. You will be her shadow. Be her. Ultimately protect her. You know I am investing all my trust in you.' He hands me a spanking new mobile device. 'Codename DV and work through glitch dates. Take a few days break first. I took it upon myself to obtain your personal items from Summertown; bank cards, passports etc. You will find them all in here.' He passes a small locked box to me, and a key. 'Usual rates and bonuses. Before you start, I'll introduce you to my backup who is covering the role at present. Sort out scheduling and time off between you.'

'You can rely on me Reginald.'

'Hm. Anything else?'

'Yes, do show me your glasses cam.'

'Oh.' He removes his glasses, blinking as he points to a miniscule lens embedded in one arm, and a microphone in the other. 'Miranda, are you sure you are fit and well for this. It is my duty to check; I am sure you understand.'

'Yes. I've been through the mire, but come out a better person. Tell me, do you know whether Summertown is available for me again?'

'I made sure, personally, that Summertown is back to rights for you. Will you head there next?'

'I will. Reginald, give my best wishes to Cynthia. It seems she and I have more in common than I originally thought.'

He doesn't reply, just flaps his hand amiably at me as if to dismiss a loyal Labrador. I know when it's time to leave. Take a final deep breath of De Vere air, and head off.

. . . .

'We have gone so far down the slippery slope of *progress*, that we all now need to call a halt. We are slaves to technology, we are polluting our planet at an alarming rate, and too many of our leaders are concerned with lining their own pockets rather than enabling hardworking citizens to thrive. Even more astounding is the emerging evidence that responsibility for the glitch lay, not with cyber-terrorists, not with the #isolators, but *with our own government*. Friends, there is a way forward …'

I run through the clip again and again, knowing what will follow, an explosion off-camera, diverting attention. Momentary darkness, followed by screaming and confusion before the camera fails, along with everything else.

That was the last time we saw Robin. Four days ago. Live-streamed to the world, on one of the hottest days of summer.

I had shadowed her, stealthily, for months, and had successfully foiled numerous attempts to discredit her. Her safety had not been compromised on my watch. I had, in Reginald's words, *known where she was every minute of the day and night*. I'm used to behaving with discretion and she appreciated my unobtrusive surveillance. Our schedule had been full-on, and she urged me to take a few days off. I reluctantly agreed. Reginald's backup bodyguard, Paul, was put in place, and on the first day, *this* happened. It's as if someone had been tracking me and saw the opportunity. Or Paul is working for them.

Supposedly *on leave*, I couldn't switch off from Robin,

and was in Summertown watching the broadcast of her latest event, so I saw it live online. Although it didn't happen while I was on duty, I feel totally responsible. Now I must employ all my skills to find her. I'm convinced there's corruption in the management of the runners. They are way too trusting, and they are being manipulated. Nathan's concept of a real-life computer game has run its course. I don't care if I am seen as the villain at Caernef. Penetrating investigation is needed.

I intend to find Robin at all costs.

Reginald is worried. He doesn't show it, but I can tell. He insists on treating Robin as a maverick daughter and cannot hide his anguish, especially as he can see that I had successfully kept her safe, religiously documenting and closing off all threats. He has confined Paul to base, pending investigations. This failure of security actually reflects well on me. But it gives me no satisfaction. I know what it's like to be imprisoned. Robin isn't as fit as I am, physically or mentally. She comes across as invincible, but it's all a front. This could break her, and without their founder and figurehead, the #isolators, the runners and the #Spoiler brigade would falter. I am consumed with the urgency of my task.

There is also a civilian investigation in train, but at a pedestrian pace. I intend to leave them far behind.

The only time that I actually saw Jennifer Hayward, was the night when she was with Reginald. From that alone, I know that she has vulnerabilities, which I may need to exploit. They managed to keep that story out of the press, so she must have strong backing in Whitehall. Reginald has given very little away, unwilling to bring that debacle back out for viewing, but my instinct tells me that Jennifer is involved in this.

A complete absence of any public online information about Jennifer Hayward convinces me further. She still works deep in Whitehall and she is said to have been the brains behind the glitch, anonymously fulfilling both the desires of her boss, and the politicians in power at the time. She was employed to pin blame on Robin's #isolators, and to discredit them at the time of the General Election. That attempt failed.

My hunch is that there is a connection between Jennifer and those infiltrating the runners. Nathan is defensive. He's meant to be looking into it for me but is dragging his heels. And all this time, Robin will be suffering. We don't even know whether she is alive. The stupid woman refused to carry a phone or an oke. They could at least track *me* most of the time, while I was in trouble, but Robin has just disappeared completely. No trace. No clues. My latest commission from De Vere Stratagems is now completely changed.

Reginald has researchers on the case. They keep sending me irrelevant details. I'm sitting at Robin's desk in the folly, trawling through endless barely relevant transcripts, hacked text messages and copied images. While I'm, briefly, at Caernef, I *have* to spend time with Nathan. He seems to be avoiding me. I mustn't be distracted with minutiae.

I stride up across the field, only one thing on my mind, but I cannot find Nathan. I scour the dormitories, check his favourite haunts, even the workshops and the allotment. No Nathan. Eventually I track him down in the dining room, eating breakfast with a group of friends, as if nothing had happened. He sees me, abandons the remnants of breakfast and hurries across. I was wrong. His face is contorted with anguish.

'Miranda. You will manage to sort this mess out, won't you?'

'Only if you help, Nathan.'

He nods. 'Let's go somewhere quiet and you can tell me what I must do.'

We walk towards the folly together, and sit on the bench overlooking the calm blue estuary. He is realising that things have rocketed out of control and, at last, is desperate to help.

'I've been worried about the ebony runners for weeks.'

'What the hell are ebony runners?'

'They started appearing in the spring, a few months ago. At first there were a few of them. Then I spotted them online, and now ... well, they're everywhere.'

'What do they do?'

'They are intent on discrediting the whole of Robin's world. They start rumours, post untrue stories, and in some cases ambush solitary runners. I'm having to instruct schedulers to deploy runners in pairs or groups, and that affects our financial sustainability. The ebony runners are openly recruiting. They are direct competition for rebellious post-millennials. It's affecting our numbers. Soon, Miranda, we are going to see a god almighty blow-up between the silver and the ebony runners. Robin would hate that.'

He shows me evidence of their online sabotage. It's subtle and it's cruel. The old *me* admires their audacity.

'Does Robin know about them?'

'No. I have only just started taking it seriously. To be honest, it's a relief to tell you about it. What are we going to do, Miranda? This might be a red herring, or they might be behind Robin's disappearance. What do you think?'

The thought that we have a tangible enemy, fires me up, even if there is no proof that they have abducted Robin.

'Where and who Nathan? I need to know.'

'All I can tell you is that they talk online of someone called Jekyll. Sometimes there's an H: Jekyll H. I don't know what or who that may be. And there's loads of activity around a remote place up in the north-west called Camp Wrath. I've had to provide the runners near there with extra protection. Oh, and I've heard them call it *Operation Isolate*.'

'Why the hell didn't you tell someone all of this earlier?'

'I'm telling *you* now aren't I?'

'Your stupid delays could have cost Robin her life.'

'Don't tell me that. I know. I'm sorry. What are you going to do?'

'Leave that to me. Concentrate on keeping the show on

the road and let me know anything... *anything* Nathan... unusual. Use the encryption. Any clues. Yes?'

Poppy skips across the parade ground, stooping to pick up treasure. She spots us, runs over, and stands behind Nathan's long legs.

Nathan nods, then withdraws a tiny parcel of tissue paper from his pocket. Inside is an Arcadian B. 'Take it, Miranda. It's a prototype, but should work well. The nano-computer inside has amazing capabilities. You will be able to stay in touch with us through this miniscule earpiece. Subtle. Do try not to lose it. I haven't received the shipment of batch one yet.

Poppy's eyes open wide.

'Shipment?'

'From Wumu Zhong.'

'Where the Fuck?'

'The factory in China.'

I pin the alluring but rather fierce bee on to my collar and stand to leave. I don't want to take Nathan with me. He would slow me down. He bows his head, still embarrassed by Robin's disappearance, allegedly masterminded by the ebony runners, but I make sure we part on good terms. I will need him onside over the next few days.

Nathan lumbers off and I am gathering my thoughts, ready to leave for an as-yet unknown place called Camp Wrath, but Poppy is still hanging around.

'Ooh Miranda, you have an Arcadian B!'

'Yes.'

'Cool. Isn't it terrible about Robin? Mummy and Daddy are so worried.'

'Aren't you worried then Poppy?'

'No. I trust in Robin. She is *invincible.*'

'I hope so.'

'She told me that word before she left for the conference.'

'Did she say anything else?'

'Yes. She kissed me on the head, here. Yuk. And she said

that she was going to escape the madness. Maybe she will go to Wumu herself. She said that one day, I could join her. That was nice wasn't it!' Poppy flashes her endearing smile at me and skips off towards the cottage, singing about Arcadian B, leaving me worrying about *Wumu*.

. . . .

Robin would certainly not have left for somewhere in China, but for the first time, prompted by Poppy, it crosses my mind that Robin has staged her exit. Her fury at the current situation is definitely intensifying. She despises the hypocrisy and hates being in the limelight. But with Caernef restored as her bolt-hole, where would she go? Surely she would have taken me into her confidence?

Not going to make the same mistakes this time: I will not go-it totally alone. I brief Reginald, telling him that I am leaving immediately for Camp Wrath, gather my kit, and head off by road, without any farewells. Can't stomach the hugs and kisses.

Despite the seriousness of the situation, I speed across Wales with renewed enthusiasm, taking advantage of the late daylight and quiet roads. Back to what I do best. It's fairly dark by the time I reach civilisation, hitting the motorway north of Chester and powering through the night. Blasting ahead as a hundred miles of M6 disappear behind me. Skirt the top of the Lake District. Music off. Compose my thoughts as I prepare for what might be one of the most important missions of my life.

It may be no coincidence that the clumsy pseudonym Jekyll H shares the initials of Jennifer Hayward. Could be a red herring. I don't think so. I'm probably being tracked. On high alert.

Miles of rural lanes until I reach the area. Location of Camp Wrath hidden like an earth. Leave the car as unobtrusively as possible. Armed with two weapons this time. Reginald's idea. One to stun. The final half-mile is best on foot. Want to see the place from above. It was deliberately blurred online, only black and white images of days as a wartime airfield with barracks and workshops. Voice in my ear from my companion bee: *approaching hostile territory.*

Never totally dark towards dawn in the height of July, and still warm outside. Easy to find my way, having memorised the map. Passing landmarks; getting close as I tread softly, skirting the forecourt of a garage for coaches, neatly parked for the night, eerily silent. Slip on to a wide path heading upwards, but then encounter the first layers of barbed wire across the track. No lights. Just the wire. Squeeze through and climb. Path becomes rocky. Reach a summit, crest the top. Now I can see Camp Wrath below me. Hope Robin isn't here as it is forbidding. Derelict buildings, lights on in a few ramshackle barracks, disused runway looking as if it is used for informal car racing. At the far end of the site, an old aerodrome building, lit up. Searchlights and scurrying people dressed in black uniforms, even at this time of night.

With a clear image of the site in my head I descend by the same route, but do not return to the car, instead am intent on gaining access through the perimeter fence. But it is clearly alarmed. I follow the fence, at a safe distance, under cover of trees and bushes. Old rusty vehicles, sand bags and oil drums. Once a disorganised place. Fly tipping and dubious debris.

Pause in a small copse twenty or so meters to the side of a main gate, which is closed and guarded. Sit on the dry ground. Watch and wait. Who are these people and what is their intention? Have they anything to do with Robin? The signs are unsurprising, "Camp Wrath, Property of HM Government: 24-hour security." Patience.

Just before dawn, a fleet of army-style trucks rumbles up the access road. As they reach the gate, I can see people sitting in the back, under the canvas covers. Black-clad and sinister. The large metal gates slide open, clanking loudly, and the parade of trucks enters. I count thirteen. That's a lot of ebony runners hidden under the canvas.

About to attempt a stealthy move into the compound, my progress is halted by another line of trucks, this time silver electric vehicles. I count eight of them, suddenly realising who they might contain. There is a bad smell around this place. Fetid air and a whiff of hypocrisy. Games are being played, possibly with Robin caught in the middle.

Noise and bustle inside Camp Wrath. Shouting, jeering and coarse laughter. More traffic approaches the gates. This time film crew, reporters, highly paid hangers-on, come for whatever spectacle has been engineered. Thinking on my feet. Fearing the worst.

Seize the opportunity and shadow the final vehicle. As it passes through the opened gate, my two small feet will be visible above the ground between the wheels. But not for long, and unseen by the guffawing guards.

They are putting on a show.

CAMP WRATH

Camp Wrath is a buzzing stage-set. I manage to slip noiselessly into one of the ramshackle store-rooms, hidden behind a stack of crates, I can see the concourse clearly, as well as two old aircraft hangers on opposite sides of the apparently disused aerodrome building. The black trucks are lined up on one side and the silver eco-vehicles on the other. Everyone seems to know what they are doing. Purposeful uniformed characters dashing here and there making preparations. For what?

Anxious in case I should become cornered in here, I make sure to have two possible exit routes available to me: back through the doorway or out through the gaping hole where there was once a window. All around the scene are similarly broken buildings. Concrete ravaged by time, overgrown railway tracks leading out past the runway and towards the sea.

I study the runners who are jumping out of the back of the vehicles and assembling on the sandy turf in front of their hanger. Their suits are too shiny, their faces too polished. The runners are behaving in an un-runner-like manner: exaggerated movements. Loud laughing. They are drinking from take-away cups and eating breakfast obtained from a silver burger van. I even spot one throwing his cup into the scrub. These are not eco-warriors. Wary, I doubt their authenticity.

The ebony runners, on the other hand, are sleek and black from head to toe. Protected by helmets and boots, they are more disciplined. They are assembling in huddles, heads together. Seemingly talking tactics. Sinister silhouettes.

Expectation is high. The ebony runners keep staring up at the aerodrome building. A heavily-clad person is handing out something. Strain my eyes. Weapons. So, the ebony runners are armed. Is this a bizarre paintball challenge. Has Nathan sent me into the heart of a weird party game?

Suddenly a voice booms from speakers, high on the aerodrome building, "Welcome combatants. Welcome to the ebony runners: the real runners. Runners with tech in their toes. Welcome too, challengers, representatives of the silver army. Runners, isolators, come to *spoil* the party."

Big Brother. Big Brother with a tinge of an accent. China? North Korea? Uncomfortable and confused, I watch the two sides assemble. They trade insults across the parade ground. Jeering.

"The countdown begins. May the strongest team win."

Massive letters are projected on to the wall of the control tower. Like New Year in New York. *Ten, nine, eight* ... as *zero* flashes, all hell breaks loose in front of my eyes. The ebony runners turn on their silver foe, brandishing laser weapons with an efficient dexterity. Silver runners try desperately to defend their ground, but falter, without guns, grabbing stones and debris to hurl at the jet-black opponents. I avert my eyes. This is a contemptuous charade.

"End of Round One." Big Brother booms. Cameras zoom. Injured bodies are retrieved, first aid administered and huddles re-form. Again, all stare up at the peeling white mortar, where a film is projected. Roars from both sides of my bolt-hole. Ebony jeering and silver wailing, as Robin's tower at Caernef is projected on to the wall. Shit, this is twisted. Parody film of dancing children on the cliff. Helicopters, bombs dropping, decimating. Runners, jet black and silver, cheer. Carnage portrayed on the peeling paint. Sinister and triumphant music blasts out, followed by an expectant silence. All eyes are turned high on the old building, where a spotlight dances, and fixes. On a small platform, behind a broken rail, we all witness the arrival of a person. A tiny silhouette high on the base of the roof. Gasps. I know that shape, being shoved out for all to see, being held precariously over the parapet, on display to the baying armies, of both sides.

"Round Two will begin. In honour of the trickster. In honour of the disruptor. In honour of the little pecking bird. Robin."

As the massive *ten* is projected up on to the wall, I dash. Through *nine and eight*, I skirt the buildings, invisible behind the ebony army. On *seven* and *six*, I am around the back of the aerodrome, eyes scanning, on complete autopilot. Up the rusted iron steps of a fire escape, up through *five* and *four*. Up through *three* and *two*. Feet on a ledge, clinging out of the reach of the lights. Loose plaster and poor handholds.

On *one*, I reach the ledge. As the klaxon sounds, and fighting resumes, I grab Robin. I grab again, my hands passing straight through her. Look high, look low, look back inside. Glimpse the laughing faces of overweight men through an upstairs window. Not laughing at me, but focused intently on the fighting below. There is no Robin. It was a sophisticated hologram, which has melted away.

…………

I have to leave this mockery. Descend the fire escape and skirt the perimeter fence, which is for show rather than security. As I am squeezing through a gap, low to the ground, I hear the rise and fall of distant raucous bellowing while the pretence of a battle continues in the aerodrome. The cacophony nearly succeeds in drowning out a closer, unfamiliar voice. Quiet, small.

'Miranda?'

'Yes.' Crawl under the barbed wire, mouth clenched against the dirt.

'Miranda, I want to talk to you?'

'I've a mouth full of mud and a pretend laser-battle at my heels. So yes, it is most convenient.'

'Oh. It's Poppy.'

'Hell! Poppy?'

'I am speaking through Arcadian B.'

'You okay?'

'I'm okay but I'm worried about Robin. You need to help.'

I crouch under a tree, with good visibility all round.

'Miranda, why have you got mud in your mouth?'

I laugh, and tell her not to worry, wiping my lips with my sleeve.

'Miranda, I was playing with my Arcadian B. It is one that Nathan didn't want any more, and when I walked past Mummy's computer, a picture came up. Robin was up high on a big building. They were going to throw her off. Miranda, you must get to her.'

I catch my breath, panting. 'Poppy, I have been up on that ledge. It is a trick, a hologram. It isn't really Robin. You mustn't worry.'

'Wow. You've actually been up there!'

'Yes. Now where is Mummy, or Daddy?'

'They are outside digging. I can see them through the window.'

'Good. You go to Mummy and Daddy and don't worry about Robin.'

'I will. Thanks Miranda. But … but where *is* Robin? She didn't go to Wumu at all.'

'I'm not sure yet. What is Wumu Poppy?'

'You know, Wumu Dong. They send us all the things, Arcadian Bs and stuff. I hear them … Oh!' She exclaims with alarm.

'What is it?'

'Miranda, I don't like this.'

'What Poppy: what?'

'Arcadian B is showing me Robin. This time it must be Robin. They are getting her ready for something. This is not a good game at all.'

'Tell me where. I can't see it.'

There is a silence. These wretched Arcadian Bs are not

perfected yet. Heaven knows how Poppy has got hold of one that works.

'Miranda, go back into that horrid place. Robin *is* there.'

Do I trust the word of a child? Despite my inbuilt reluctance to trust anyone, I find my legs returning towards the aerodrome. Grip my pair of weapons. One to kill and one to stun. Prepared. Speed. Under the wire.

'Miranda, I can see it all: go into the door at the back of the big building. Go straight up the stairs. Robin is in a room at the front. They are getting her ready for something terrible.'

Locate the door. Unguarded and unlocked. These game-players haven't got a grip on real-life security. Head up the stairs.

'Poppy what are you doing there? Put that thing down. I've warned you about fiddling with it too close to the computer.' Maria. In from the garden. A click in my ear. Dead line.

Poppy said a room at the front. Rushing blindly, I follow the sound of raised voices. Robin's voice. I am sure. Furious.

'I will *not* cooperate with such a ridiculous and damaging trick. I will not do it.'

Screams of agony.

Stealth. I sidle up to the half-open door and peer inside. Jennifer Hayward has her clothes on this time, and is flanked by four bodyguards, each restraining Robin. The real Robin. And a woman filming, grinning inanely as Robin struggles, blood pouring from a cut on her face. Not stage-blood.

Mask over my face. Precision required. Without thinking, I select the stun gun and shoot. Jennifer first. As Jekyll H falls, they panic. I get three of them. Robin breaks free. The grinning camera woman films throughout. I aim at the final bodyguard, but miss as he is quick. No matter as Robin is beside me. Grab her hand. Fingerless gloved hand, like when she rescued me from the streets.

By the time the alarms and klaxons are splitting the air, I have guided Robin out of the building. We are scrabbling under the loose barbed wire. *Run, run as fast as you can. You can't catch me I'm the gingerbread man.*

Arcadian B vibrates on my chest. As we run, Robin panting, Maria's voice, "Miranda can you hear me?"

'Yes'

"Reginald is sending a helicopter. Right now. Take cover, wait.'

We dive under a hedge along the edge of a large field of sheep. Camp Wrath too close for comfort. Robin squeezes my hand, and holds her sleeve over the cut on her face, 'Thanks Miranda. How on earth did you know where to find me?'

'Don't thank me yet. We aren't safe …'

We hear distant rotor blades. Simultaneously the engines of jeeps roar into action inside Cape Wrath.

'Despicable people.'

'Who are they Robin?'

'They are the new generation of cyberthugs, sponsored by businesses in China to disrupt the #isolator supply chains. They are playing the game of life, turning it into a lurid spectacle. I hate them, Miranda. I hate them.'

The helicopter seems to take so long. A dot in the sky becomes a gnat, becomes a fly, but the jeeps are gaining ground.

'I shot Jennifer Hayward.'

'So that's who she was.'

'Is. It was only a stun gun. Not making that mistake again. But if those jeeps reach us, I *will* shoot.'

'Who would have thought, on that night in The Pike, that the enigmatic Miranda would save my life, several times over.'

'You saved mine: remember.'

The helicopter circles above our heads. The pilot selects a spot, and descends. Too loud to speak now. Hatch opens and we rush in. I glance back to see the first jeep reach the field. The camerawoman, silently shooting footage. Social media: mankind's new weapon. Still grinning, she waves.

'It's all a game to them.'

'We need another glitch. Knock them out.'

....

For a brief moment I wonder whether this is a set-up too, and the helicopter has been despatched by Chinese capitalism, or renegade real-life wargamers, but I glimpse a familiar pair of jacketed shoulders beside the pilot.

'Reginald!'

'Miranda, and Robin. My two favourite girls.' We grimace.

'Reginald, you don't often come out on a mission yourself.'

'I couldn't resist this one. We were standing by within range. What a fascinating battle of wits. Tell me, Miranda, *was* it Jennifer in there?'

'It was. And I shot her with the stun. That was a good idea of yours.'

Robin is receiving first aid, but she doesn't hold back, 'You are as bad as each other. Turning life into some sort of fun fest. Glorified cops and robbers twenty-first century style. They are despicable people. Did you see what they called me: *little pecking bird*. While we are sailing the skies, burning hundreds of pounds worth of fuel, people are starving. The planet is being strangled. Not slowly. And they spend their time goading others, mimicking and demeaning. Why won't they simply leave our runners alone. And who *are* those ebony characters?'

'Nathan tipped me off about them: the ebony runners. Apparently they are seriously threatening #isolate.'

Reginald interrupts her, 'Ebony runners. I read about them in the draft legislation. Saw it yesterday. The government is not hanging around.'

This is news to me. As usual, Reginald is several steps ahead, 'What legislation Reginald? What's going on back in Westminster?'

'Not only in Westminster, but in each of the four nations. Robin's silver runners are to be protected by law. Providing a vital service to local communities in challenging times. Open competition will be prohibited. It actually mentions groups such as ebony runners. They will go underground, of course … and another thing, we must recall all those epods. Robin you need to step up your due diligence on the technology. Apparently the state-run Chinese business is manufacturing the epods: the ones used by runners to scan receipt of goods …'

'and to convey secret messages between #isolators …'

'… and that … they are dependent on a Chinese technology which allows the original owners of the software to view all communications. Fed directly into their marketing strategies, and helped them to establish the ebony brigade.'

'And no doubt fuel their ongoing surveillance.'

'No doubt.'

I stretch out in the back of the helicopter, half-listening to the conversation between Robin and Reginald, and I reflect how close I have brushed with total failure over the last year. But now, as the helicopter descends, and I realise my car is left up in the north west, I am right in the centre again. Accepted. Trusted. Valued.

'Miranda, you were amazing.'

'Just doing my job. Actually, it's Poppy who you should thank.'

'Poppy?'

…………

Caernef in deep summer. Robin and I are walking back down towards the folly after breakfast. Nathan hurtles across the field carrying a bundle of wires tangled with antennae. He trips, metal objects go flying into the scrubby grass, and he swears, scrabbling around, picking up the spilt parts. Robin spots him and pounces, her voice tinged with acrimony.

'Nathan Price. You'd be better leaving it all to rust in the grass. It would do less harm that way.'

'Robin! Miranda! You're back. What do you mean? It won't rust anyway.'

'I'm back, no thanks to you, having been thrust into yet another of your cruel cybergames. You knew about the ebony runners, didn't you?'

'I only just discovered them …'

'You set it up. In that horrendous Camp Wrath. Your game-playing has gone too far this time.'

'What do you mean?'

'*My* runners don't need you and your …'

'*Your* runners … they are *my* runners remember?'

Robin ignores his repost and looms over him, hands on her hips in the way she stands when she is furious.

'Your ecopods must go. Such a great device, you said. Magically connect up the #isolators, you said. Well Nathan, what you didn't know … what you didn't know, was that the Chinese retained the legal rights to view us through *your* supposedly cutting-edge gear. All the while we thought that we were controlling the most innovative technology enabling the eco-revolution, we were feeding intelligence to *them*.'

'I did suspect. They insisted on the inclusion of so many cyber-intelligence clauses.'

'You suspected! Then it is even worse than I thought.'

Robin's voice is as cold as steel, and, despite everything he has done, she cuts him loose.

'Nathan, you're fired. Today. You will leave all your equipment behind, including phones, ecopods and your Arcadian B controller. You will no longer play any part in Caernef, or *my* runners, in #isolate, or in #Spoiler. I will not be instigating any repayment clauses, but you will hear from my lawyers. Leave me with an address. By midnight tonight Nathan. Go.'

With an uncharacteristic glint of fury in his eyes, rather than regret, Nathan glares, speechless, turns his back on us and strides off, chucking his collection of Arcadian antennae across the grass.

Our debrief is prevented by Poppy, innocently skipping across the tussocks towards us, waving a newspaper, which she hands to me with trembling fingers.

'What does it mean Miranda?'

Leaning on my arm, it is Robin who reads the headline aloud, *Major compromise of UK Government intelligence believed to originate in Wumu Zhong, China.* Underneath is a photograph of Reginald, handcuffed, entitled *Codename Reddleman: Cover blown.*

....

'I was always nervous of Reginald. I mean, you could never be sure whether he was on your side or theirs. Was he part of the old government, and did he actually understand #isolate?' Robin is musing,

'I would have given my life for him,' I reflect.

'Miranda, I was too hasty with Nathan, wasn't I?'

'Yes. You owe him. The runners, the earths, the okes, Arcadian B … he has invested a great deal in Caernef and in #isolate. You were too hasty.'

'We all make mistakes. I simply need to put it right. Has he left yet?'

'I don't think so.'

'Would you find him for me?'

I leave Robin on the bench at the foot of the folly, the window in the lookout reflecting the sunset, and again, find myself searching for Nathan. Wisps of thin smoke are dancing in the direction of his workshop. I walk through the soft evening light, to find a forlorn figure poking an incinerator, ash billowing into the air. He is deep in thought, and doesn't see me approach.

'Nathan?'

'Oh, Miranda. Look. This is the last of Robin's inheritance. The stash from the attic in the folly. Those terrorists set fire to it, over two years ago now. I kept the last few bundles in a sack. They were only singed. No use now. Don't worry. If she has sent you to check, I'm packed up and will be off as soon as Gid has had supper. He has offered to drop me at the station.'

'Is that what you want?'

'No. But I messed up. Robin is right. Time I left.'

He turns away in an attempt to hide his wet eyes from me. 'Robin can be hot-headed sometimes. Truth is, she needs you here. She wants you here. She can't do this without you Nathan.'

For a moment his face lightens, 'Really?'

'Yes. Now come and have a chat with her. Can you do that?'

'I don't know. What do you think Miranda?'

I gaze out to sea, and then I study Nathan's troubled face. 'We all make mistakes. What really matters is how we move on from them.'

Chris Malone

BOOK 3: #FUTUREPROOF

June 2034, Poppy

Caernef is the only home which I have known. It has been a strange upbringing, immersed in a counter-culture, roaming the headlands alone, collecting specimens. I have been sheltered from the realities of the streets, out on our remote headland, and yet hooked-in to the espionage which has always surrounded Miranda and Robin, the invincible puppet-masters. Chalk and cheese. Robin, venerable and wise, with insights which astound us all, and Miranda, who sweeps you up in a veil of intrigue and never quite allows you to see the goodness in it. Robin trusts. Robin listens, reassures and cares with a passion that seems to increase as she grows increasingly frail. But Miranda is wicked. Just downright wicked.

My parents want the best for me, but they simply don't understand. They tell me, on a daily basis, to ignore Miranda, not to become caught up in her world. But I watch them watching me, as I am pulled magnetically into Miranda's aura. She's a survivor, sharp, and fleet of foot. She always beats me in the water and over rough terrain, but tells me *not for long*. She jokes that, when she and Robin retire gracefully, I am next in line, so I must train hard. It's not a joke to me. It's deadly serious, but I don't fit her stereotype. I try, but I'm not built for it.

Mum and Dad want me to stay at home, and focus on my studies, on the camp, and on building a respectable future, like Cai, the model and dutiful brother, who does everything right. But I see the sadness in their eyes, as with trepidation, they try to understand my passion for *her* ways. They tell me to sit with *Robin*, out on the rocks overlooking the estuary, because she holds the wisdom which we all seek. But I am desperate to earn one of Miranda's rare smiles, when she eventually turns up, which isn't often these days.

My friends from school are content living in virtuality most of the time. They don't understand why I take such a strong stand against it, but Robin's words rattle in my head, *human beings were not made to exist through their fingertips, attached to artificial devices. Put it away Poppy. Put it away.*

So, I sacrificed the gameplay. I sacrificed the reward stakes and the virtual friends. The trouble is that when you see it all from the outside, the sham complicity is so obvious. Where others exist in their created worlds as perfect human beings, sculpted using hi-tech apps and the most expensive character-building software, I remain rough and ready. Short and plump, with real mud on my shoes and wind in my hair. I know I will never be a superhero like Miranda and so I worry, secretly.

Nathan Price has made his zillions on the back of people's desire to be different. Their quest for the perfect identity fulfilled. Genius rewarded Miranda says. But I remember the day of the great split, and it wasn't pretty. He was always kind to me, Nathan. He used to give me his prototypes to play with and listened to my ideas for new gadgets and gismos. Arcadian B was the best of all, back in the early days, when I wasn't tall enough to reach his designing bench, and had to stand on a wooden box. I remember him handing me the beautiful silver bee, saying that he had received it from China, but that it wasn't activated. However, I soon realised that my Arcadian B had powers.

The great split came soon after I used his silver gizmo to help Miranda, who was courageously rescuing Robin from capture. That was the beginning of my lifelong bond with Miranda. It was the day before I witnessed Robin throw Nathan out, forever.

I was playing quietly behind the herb beds at Caernef, small for a six-year-old, and dwarfed by the culinary jungle. As it was deep summer, the foliage was high and fragrant: deep bushed fennel and dry wispy quaking grass, which rattled if you brushed past. I was totally hidden from view. It was a chance meeting, as Robin and Miranda were walking back down towards the folly after breakfast, and Nathan was hurtling across the field carrying a bundle of wires and antennae. He tripped, and metal objects went flying into the scrubby grass. He swore, and scrabbled around picking the bits up.

It was then that Robin fired him. Told him to go from Caernef forever. I was shocked.

As the distraught figures disappeared over the field, I ran home to tell Cai what I had heard.

That was ten years ago, and ironically it was the making of Nathan. He stayed for a while, but eventually set up independently and registered all his new software under the *virtuality* brand. Miranda says good on him for taking the opportunity. Now he's a zillionaire and owns the biggest virtual reality platform on the planet. He even offered me a role in his character-design studio in the school holidays, but I declined, politely. That's not where my interests lie.

Chris Malone

ABOUT THE AUTHOR

Chris started her career cleaning toilets in a local outdoor centre for schools, while she studied for her degree with the Open University. Thirty-five years later she was Head of Education in Warwickshire. Now enjoying her retirement, having relocated to Herefordshire, Chris is an avid nature enthusiast.

When she's not rewilding the garden or writing novels, she's catching up on re-reading all her favourite dystopian titles and classic novels. #isolate is a standalone thriller set around the time of the 2024 general election. It follows on from #stoptheglitch, her second novel, with #FutureProof set to complete the glitch trilogy.

Chris Malone

More Titles From Burton Mayers Books you might like:

Post-pandemic
dependence on tech
is shattered by the
glitch, a cyber-attack,
which temporarily
knocks out power and
communication
networks.

£7.99 UK

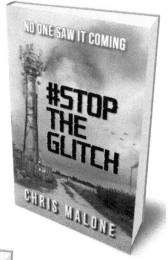

A fast-paced blend
of science fiction
and historical fiction
interwoven into an
ancestral, time-travel
mystery.

£7.99 UK

Lightning Source UK Ltd.
Milton Keynes UK
UKHW011100110921
390284UK00002B/39